SPLATT

SPLATT

A SINGLE DROP THAT CHANGED AN OCEAN

DANIEL GROENEWALD

Daniel Groenewald
www.danielgroenewald.com

INTRODUCTION

This book is a conversion from a screenplay. To retain some of the original feel of the screenplay, certain features have been kept. Location headings are provided for each change in location, and at times cameras zooming in or out are mentioned. Also, the character dialogue appears line by line in a screenplay format.

PROLOGUE

It's strange that the third planet from the sun is called "Earth" and not "Oceana." After all, water covers more than two-thirds of the Earth's surface. And all that water, at some point in time, consisted of individual drops. Equally strange is that water absorbs the colors of the light spectrum at various depths, making them no longer visible. First to disappear is red at around three meters, then orange at five, followed by yellow at seven, green at twenty-two, and finally blue at about sixty-five meters. Below that everything appears in shades of grey, and anything living at that depth would be blissfully unaware that color exists and what it looks like.

It is at one hundred meters below the surface that a community of drops reside. Their village is nestled between two large rocks that offer good protection from ocean currents. They call themselves Sea Drops, and Splatt, a curious and slightly rebellious drop, is one of them. He has heard forbidden rumors that color exists. No one knows the origin of these rumors. But away from prying ears, whispers suggest that all is not grey.

OCEAN FLOOR, MORNING

SPLATT walks the ocean floor. He has a funky, gelled hairstyle—brushed forward and turned up in the front. His transparent little body is grey like everything else at this depth, including the seemingly giant-sized fish swimming overhead. But his focus is less on the fish overhead, and more on finding the Ink Fish. He comes across a spiral shell ten times his own size and attempts to lift it. He fails. Frustrated, and in an obvious hurry, he scouts for a smaller shell and eventually finds one about half his size. With much heaving and groaning, he manages to lift it and smash it on a nearby rock, keeping for himself the bottom end of the cone. This feat gives him confidence, and he relaxes. He thinks out loud.

> SPLATT
> (with a determined frown)
> I'm coming for you, Mister Ink Fish. I know where you hide out. Today I'll get some ink from you.

But his confidence is short lived and turns to fear when he suddenly looks up and realizes the size of the ocean creatures above him.

SPLATT
(in shaky voice)
Go, boy … it'll be worth it.

He is clearly unfamiliar with his surroundings, and he is visibly scared. He trembles as he creeps up a canyon. Ahead of him is a single sucker that dwarfs him. He cowers as if he knows that the ring means danger. Zooming out shows the sucker to be one of an array on a giant tentacle, and a further zoom out shows the colossal Ink Fish in front of the tiny Splatt. Panicked, Splatt turns on his heels to run, but something catches his eye—a trickle of black ink some ten paces to his left. Indecisive, for a moment he stands trembling, then he darts to the ink and nervously fills up his cone with it before running away frantically. He carefully preserves what's left in the cone once he's out of harm's way.

In the distance we see Splatt's village, Sea Drop Village, which is constructed from pebbles, coral, and whole or broken seashells, with a scattering of kelp and seaweed. Splatt sees the grey outline of his school campus in the distance and cringes. The camera pans to the school's entrance to reveal an arch with the school's name, its teachers, and their subjects:

SEA DROP HIGH SCHOOL
Principal—Mr. Schooner
Sea Drop Orientation—Miss Barge
Religious Instruction—Miss Barge

CLASSROOM, MORNING

Drops of water (all grey) are in their underwater classroom. They sit at perfectly spaced desks in utter silence. The rows are spaced boy/girl alternately. The boy and girl drops have the same hairstyles respectively—platted pigtails for girls and side partings for boys. The individual Drops can, however, be distinguished by their facial features. At the back of the second row of boys' desks is an empty desk and chair.

> MISS BARGE, a Drop of considerable weight and an obvious spinster, addresses the class in a highfalutin, almost lyrical tone.

MISS BARGE
Good morning, class.

CLASS
Morning, ma'am.

MISS BARGE
You all know my name is Miss Barge, and it has been a pleasure—no, a privilege—to have been able to teach Sea Drop Orientation to you for the last four years. This is your last school year, and next year you

should be able to take your places in society as adults and hopefully worthy Sea Drops. You are now the big fish in a small pond, but next year you will be the small fish in a big pond, if you'll excuse the pun.

She laughs at her own weak joke, but the class clearly doesn't think she's funny.

MISS BARGE
(in a more serious tone)

In any event, as I was saying, you are not Droplets anymore, you are now young adult Drops … on the verge of taking on the responsibilities of worthy Sea Drops. And I, I am but a tool in the hands of the Creator to guide you on your path, to prepare you for the challenges and … the difficulties that come with adulthood and with being worthy Sea Drops.

OCEAN FLOOR, MORNING

Splatt is in the home stretch. He is completely out of breath and starts walking as he reaches the outskirts of Sea Drop Village. From here a sandy footpath winds past dwellings to the pebble arch that is the school's entrance. Next to the footpath lies a bright red drop that looks exactly like Splatt, except he is red.

The red drop has both his hands cupped behind his head and his thin tentacle-like legs crossed. He looks very content. Splatt sees him and stops.

> SPLATT
> (staring at him in disbelief)
> I've never seen anything like this. Are you from the Land of Color?

> RED DROP
> You mean Colorland? Maybe I am.

> SPLATT
> Your color, what's it called?

> RED DROP
> I'm red.

SPLATT
Wow, red is awesome. Where is it, then?

RED DROP
Where's what?

SPLATT
The Land of Color, man … um … Colorland. Where is it? I'm late for class.

CLASSROOM, MORNING

MISS BARGE
Now class, let me begin by individually greeting each one of you. Please … *please* do not think of this as roll call, but rather as a rekindling of friendships after the holiday. I'm quite sure that all of us are perfectly adult enough to know that attending this class is not a duty nor a chore, but a beautiful privilege.

Miss Barge picks up a sheet of seaweed paper and starts to call the roll. The camera slowly pans to an empty chair and desk at the back of the class.

MISS BARGE
Sarah Drop.

From the second row, second from the front, a little tentacle arm shoots up.

SARAH
Present, ma'am.

MISS BARGE
Anthony Drop.

ANTHONY
Present, ma'am.

OCEAN FLOOR, MORNING

SPLATT
Where is it? Quickly—I told you I'm late.

RED DROP
Where is it. Well, you … you sort of need to find your own way there.

SPLATT
How?

RED DROP
Maybe you can start by letting go of the way you know.

CLASSROOM, MORNING

MISS BARGE
Mathew Drop.

MATHEW
Present, ma'am.

MISS BARGE
Christine Drop.

CHRISTINE
Present, ma'am.

MISS BARGE
Joseph Drop.

JOSEPH
Present, ma'am.

MISS BARGE
Lara Drop.

LARA blushes. She's uncomfortable with the empty desk and chair beside her.

LARA
(whispering)
Present, ma'am.

PASSAGE LEADING TO CLASSROOM, MORNING

Splatt runs down the passage. He stops in front of the door and pulls a comb from behind his back. He changes his funky hairstyle to the same-side parting that the rest of the class have.

CLASSROOM, MORNING

MISS BARGE
Spl— What in heaven's name? Surely Jonathan has grown up enough to let go of this ridiculous name, Splatt … Splatt?

The class giggles.

MISS BARGE
Splatt J. Drop.

The door bursts open. Splatt runs to his desk and crashes onto his chair. He then looks up, composed as though he had been there all the time, and answers the roll call.

SPLATT
Present, ma'am.

The class giggles. Miss Barge walks to Splatt's desk. He quickly hides the ink behind his back.

MISS BARGE
What is your name, boy?

SPLATT
Splatt, ma'am.

MISS BARGE
Splatt?

SPLATT
That's right.

MISS BARGE
That's right, who?

SPLATT
That's right … ma'am.

MISS BARGE
All right then, Splatt … tell me this—why have I known you for four years as Jonathan Drop?

SPLATT
That's my christened name, ma'am, but I choose to—

MISS BARGE
Splatt … Splatt … Where in Thunder God's Sea does "Splatt" come from with a beautiful name like Jonathan? What's the matter with you, boy?

SPLATT
Nothing, ma'am. It's just that—

MISS BARGE
It's just that nothing.

Miss Barge turns and addresses the class.

MISS BARGE
I can smell a rotten oyster from a mile away. Beware, class. It is said that too many cooks spoil the broth, but I say it only takes one rotten oyster to spoil the broth.

Miss Barge walks back to the front of the class. She talks to the class while Splatt tries to get Lara's attention.

MISS BARGE
Class, pay no attention to Jonathan Drop's antics.

SPLATT
(whispering)
Psst, Lara. Lara! Psst!

MISS BARGE
We know the way to true freedom is through discipline …

LARA
(interrupting Splatt's persistent "pssts")
Wait, Splatt.

MISS BARGE
… and discipline comes through sacrifice. Sacrifice is the one thing that we have to learn. A Sea Drop's life is not his …

SPLATT
(to Lara)
Hey, I got something for you.

MISS BARGE
… own, only by the grace of Thunder God. … Only by His grace do we exist, and our purpose is to His glory.

LARA
W…a…i…t, Splatt.

Splatt produces the cone of ink from behind his back and tries to sneak it to Lara.

MISS BARGE
Jonathan Drop—what is that?

Miss Barge walks slowly and purposefully to Splatt's desk and towers over him.

MISS BARGE
Hand it over, boy.

Splatt has the cone behind his back.

MISS BARGE
I said hand it over, boy!

Splatt produces the cone and hands it over to Miss Barge.

MISS BARGE
What is this?

SPLATT
Ink, ma'am.

MISS BARGE
Ink? Ink from where?

Silence.

MISS BARGE
Ink from where, boy? You're testing my patience.

SPLATT
From the open ocean, ma'am.

MISS BARGE
I was not mistaken, you are a rotten oyster. What kind of example is this to your classmates?

She turns and addresses the class.

MISS BARGE
Class, "Splatt" (the name said sarcastically) was very lucky indeed to get away with this. I guarantee you it was the exception—the open ocean is filled not only with fish but also with all manner of ghastly creatures, any of which will not hesitate to swallow you—in fact they will not even be aware that they have done so. And this, you know, would spell a torturous end to your existence.

Miss Barge turns back to Splatt.

MISS BARGE
Get rid of that ink. Get rid of it immediately. I will not have it in my class. Take it to the waste disposal

room. Take it now. … In heaven's name, the audacity. … To think that you would be so brazen as to bring the evidence of your transgression into my classroom. Get rid of it.

Splatt leaves the classroom with shoulders drooping.

PASSAGE, MORNING

Splatt walks past a room marked "STAFF TEA ROOM." (There's chatter from inside.) Then he walks past the door marked "PRINCIPAL—Mr. Schooner." (He cringes.) Finally, he reaches the room marked "WASTE DISPOSAL." He reaches for the doorknob but changes his mind. He rushes outside and hides the ink by half-burying it behind a rock.

CLASSROOM, MORNING

Splatt returns and takes his place at his desk. The bell rings. Drops start packing up feverishly.

MISS BARGE

Not so quick, class. Before you go to break—two things. First, your homework: you will read the first chapter of your prescribed book *Success Through Discipline*. And second: Jonathan Drop, you will come to this classroom after school today, and you will write out on the greenboard, "I will never go into the open ocean again" … three hundred times.

The class gasps.

MISS BARGE

Let this be an example to all of you. That will be all for now, boys and girls. You may go.

SCHOOLYARD, MORNING

Splatt is standing on a small rock. He addresses a couple of boys.

SPLATT
One of its tentacles is bigger than our entire school, I tell you, he's scary.

BOY FROM THE GROUP
So, how'd ya get the ink?

SPLATT
I just went straight for his ink gland. I tell you, it's the size of a house. So, I just punched him there—right there in the gland. I think I hurt him… 'cause he got scared. Ink Fish only squirt ink when they're scared, you know. And then… then from this ginormous gland he squirted a stream of ink like… like you've never seen.

ANOTHER BOY FROM THE GROUP
Weren't you scared, Splatt?

SPLATT
Na… not me. I tell you what—to get that ink from that stream, now *that* was dangerous. Dangerous, the force—eesh, it was too much.

BOY FROM THE GROUP
Awesome!

The boys are looking up at Splatt, and they don't realize that Lara is within earshot behind Splatt.

SPLATT
Then … then the fish starts squirming with pain. And the currents … phew!

BOY FROM THE GROUP
Wow, what did you do then?

SPLATT
Me … I just hung on. It was tough, but I hung on.

LARA
(from behind Splatt)
You did all this just to get me some ink, Splatt?

Splatt climbs off the rock. He becomes all coy. He walks over to Lara where the boys can't hear him.

SPLATT
It was really nothing. It actually wasn't like that. I just wanted to bring back some ink for you as proof that I was out there in the open ocean, and that it's not as

dangerous as they tell us. I guess, in a way I was also hoping to see color—something none of us has ever seen. That is, until now.

Silence for a while. Splatt waits for Lara to respond, but she doesn't.

SPLATT
You see, all I got out there was black ink to show you. But—and listen to this—on my way back, something very strange happened. It felt like a dream, but I'm pretty sure it wasn't. I saw a Color Drop. I was bowled over. He said he was the color red. Red is the most beautiful thing I've ever seen, except … Splatt looks down and slowly rises his gaze from Lara's feet to her eyes, hinting that it's Lara that's more beautiful than red.

LARA
(unaware of the hint)
Except what?

SPLATT
Except um … nothing. Lara, I know it's not supposed to be, and what they say and all that … but I saw it, Lara—with my own eyes, I swear to you. I don't think I was dreaming. I saw it.

LARA
Splatt, don't!

SPLATT
But it's true, Lara. He said he's from the Land of Color. The place even has a name: Colorland—that's what he called it. I think … I think there might be another side to what they're teaching us here. Maybe they're lying to us. Maybe there *is* a Land of Color. Just maybe, Colorland really exists.

LARA
Maybe, but I don't want to know.

The bell rings. The drops make their way back to the classroom.

CLASSROOM, AFTERNOON

Splatt picks up the coral-chalk marker and begins writing his punishment on the greenboard, fashioned from flattened seaweed. After writing only two lines, he becomes distracted and starts daydreaming. Suddenly he perks up as though a light has been switched on in his mind. He sneaks down the passage past the staff tearoom (chatter again) and past the principal's office. He retrieves the ink and almost gets caught on his way back when the principal's door opens unexpectedly. The principal, MR SCHOONER, is seeing someone off. Splatt, without having seen Mr. Schooner or his guest, just makes it out of sight and into the waste disposal room, where he hides. He overhears the conversation outside.

> PRINCIPAL SCHOONER
> I assure you we will eradicate this cancer that Johnathan has started before it spreads, Miss Barge. You have my full support. We cannot allow this.

> MISS BARGE
> Thank you, Principal Schooner.

Splatt is shaking. He hears doors shut and waits in silence until the coast is clear. He contemplates putting the ink in the waste disposer, but he gains confidence and makes his way back to the classroom. Once back in the classroom, he faces the almost insurmountable task ahead of him as he stares at the greenboard. He then hears his prior conversation with the red drop in his mind.

> RED DROP
> Where is it? Well, you … you sort of need to find your own way there.
>
> SPLATT
> How?
>
> RED DROP
> Maybe you can start by letting go of the way you know.

He puts his finger in the ink and writes the next line on the greenboard in ink, "I must let go of the way I know."

He reaches for the eraser and brings it to rest on the writing. A conflict clearly develops within him. Finally, he attempts to erase it—but it smudges. He tries to undo what he did, but his best attempts fail, and the words he wrote can clearly be seen through the smudge.

He tries to overwrite the words with "I will never go into the open ocean again," but the ink writing shines through. Finally, he erases all the coral-chalk writing and leaves only the smudged ink. He exits the class.

LARA'S BEDROOM, AFTERNOON

Lara is doing her homework at her desk. From her second-floor window, she sees Splatt passing by on his way home.

> LARA
> (excited)
> Splatt!

Splatt looks up and waves sheepishly.

> LARA
> Wait for me, Splatt.

Splatt produces a comb and fashions his hair into the funky style, just in time before Lara meets him on the pavement.

> LARA
> So?

> SPLATT
> Hi.

LARA
Have you finished?

SPLATT
What?

LARA
Your punishment, silly.

SPLATT
Mm, well … yes … sort of.

An uncomfortable silence follows.

PASSAGE, AFTERNOON

Miss Barge exits the principal's office and makes her way down the passage to her classroom, expecting to find Splatt doing his punishment. She sees the mess on the greenboard. She's furious.

OUTSIDE LARA'S HOUSE, AFTERNOON

LARA
What do you mean, "sort of?"

SPLATT
Lara?

LARA
Yes?

SPLATT
Do you think that there is a Land of Color?

LARA
Stop it, Splatt.

SPLATT
(excited)
No, listen to me. I swear … that Color Drop … a bright red one. Lara, what if … What if …

LARA
What if what?

SPLATT

What if it's all a lie? What if there is a Land of Color? You know, when I was out there this morning … in the open ocean … You see, Lara, they tell us not to go beyond anything here, and yes, I was scared. I was scared out there this morning, I was petrified, but nothing happened. I think they're just scaring us. I think it's all just one big lie.

LARA

What?

SPLATT

Everything, Lara. Everything … they warn us that if we go into the open ocean, fish will swallow us. They teach us that Thunder God that will punish us if we transgress their rules. I also wonder if we really are so special because we're Sea Drops. I'm even questioning the ultimate transgression—to rise to the surface. I think it's all a lie. You should have seen it out there—it's beautiful—stunning.

LARA

You know we're not really supposed to discuss any of this. And yes, you may be right about certain things. But there's one thing that I know to be true and cannot be convinced otherwise: the surface … we all know what that means—evaporation, death by being pulled apart.

SPLATT
Am I the only one around here who's willing to challenge what we're taught here? What if evaporation doesn't kill us?

LARA
There are certain things that one cannot question.

SPLATT
Why not?

LARA
I don't know.

SPLATT
Precisely. You don't know. Just think of this a bit. I want to know everything. Everything!

Lara thinks a while.

LARA
Actually, Splatt, I think you're brave, yes, very brave. You brave it out into the open ocean to ... and you want to know about things that no one ... I think you're brave.

Embarrassed, Splatt smiles.

SPLATT
I got to go. I got stuff to ... to think about.

SPLATT'S HOUSE, DUSK

Splatt walks from the gate in the seashell fence to the front door. He lets himself in. He hears his father's (LIONEL) voice—it approaches and becomes louder.

> LIONEL
> Is that you, Jonathan? Where have you been all aftern—

Splatt desperately fumbles for his comb to correct his hairstyle, but it's too late. His father rounds the corner.

> LIONEL
> How many times have I warned you about that hairstyle, boy?

Splatt looks to the ground.

> LIONEL
> Look at me when I speak to you, boy. How many times?

Splatt looks up but does not answer. He is frightened.

> LIONEL
> You just won't listen now, will you? You think you're different now, don't you? Well, I'll show you how

different you are. Go to your room and wait for me. I'll show you what different gets you.

Splatt walks up the stairs to his bedroom. He has found his comb and starts to comb his hair correctly.

LIONEL
(shouting from behind him)
It's too late now, boy. You should have thought of this before you combed that rebel style.

SPLATT'S HOUSE, IN THE LOUNGE, EVENING

Splatt's mother (ELAINE) is sitting in the lounge. Lionel walks in and sits down.

ELAINE
Lionel?

LIONEL
Yes?

ELAINE
Why are you so hard on Jonathan?

LIONEL
I'm not.

ELAINE
He's not a boy anymore, you know.

LIONEL
(indignant)
Hmm.

ELAINE
It's not that he means to be—

LIONEL
(interrupting)
Elaine!

ELAINE
Please hear me out, Lionel. It's just that I think—

LIONEL
Elaine. You're starting to annoy me, Elaine.

ELAINE
Sorry, dear.

LIONEL
I'll tell you what's wrong with your boy. It's simple … easy … anyone can understand it. He's a disobedient rebel. That's what he is, plain and simple, a disobedient rebel.

ELAINE
Yes, dear.

LIONEL
All he needs is some discipline—that's all.

Elaine freezes.

ELAINE
Why, for the way he combs his hair?

LIONEL
You're starting to annoy me again, Elaine.

SPLATT'S BEDROOM, EVENING

Splatt sits in front of the mirror. He combs his hair into the correct style. In his mind he hears his father's voice, "It's too late now, boy." Then he remembers his conversation with the Color Drop. "How do you get there? Well, you … you sort of need to find your own way there." "How?" "Maybe you can start by letting go of the way you know."

Splatt reverses his hairstyle back to funky. The door opens. His father enters the room.

> LIONEL
> Did I not tell you to comb your … *Elaine*! Elaine, come here and look at your son.

> SPLATT
> (scared)
> But Dad, you said it was too late now, that—

> LIONEL
> What? Are you a moron? Are you stupid? Do you have no brains? Of course, you have no brains—no brains can develop under that rebel hairstyle now, can they?

Elaine enters the room.

ELAINE
Lionel, calm down.

LIONEL
Calm down? I have a good mind to …

Lionel lifts his hand as if to strike Splatt. Splatt ducks.

LIONEL
You will not wear that hairstyle under my roof—is that *clear*? *Fix it!*

Splatt nervously fixes his hair.

LIONEL
That's better. Now listen to me, boy. You're testing my limits …

ELAINE
Lionel, it was Jonathan's first day back at school, don't …

LIONEL
Be quiet, you're really starting to annoy me now. And that reminds me—your child's last report card mentioned his tendency to be rebellious.

Lionel turns to Splatt.

LIONEL
And you, boy, you're almost big now. I don't know how that happened, 'cause you're like a kid with that

hairstyle. Don't embarrass me with your rebellion. Don't! Do you hear me, boy? Or else I will—

Lionel lifts his hand again. Splatt. Splatt cringes.

ELAINE
No, Lionel!

LIONEL
Wait. I'm thinking.

Splatt is obviously nervous as Lionel ponders.

LIONEL
You're lucky, boy. … You're lucky I'm in a good mood.

LARA'S HOUSE, IN THE LOUNGE, EVENING

Lara is sitting with her parents (LEN and CATHARINE). The lounge is neat and tidy.

LARA
Mum, Dad …

CATHARINE
Yes, sweetie?

LARA
Nothing.

CATHARINE
What is it, deary?

LARA
Well, I don't know that I should be discussing this.

LEN
(with a stern voice)
Lara, you know that you can discuss anything with your mother and me. Now what's on your mind?

LARA
I know, Daddy. … Well, it's Splatt. He seems to think he saw a Color Drop, and I was wondering—

LEN
That's nonsense. They don't exist.

CATHARINE
How can you just state that as fact, Len?

LEN
Well, everyone is entitled to his or her own opinion, and that includes me.

CATHARINE
Opinion, yes. … Well, I think—that is, in my opinion—we just cannot rule it out simply because we haven't seen it. As everyone is entitled to their own opinion, so everyone is responsible for their own path wherever it may lead. And if someone wishes to investigate Color Drops or even whether a Colorland exists, they should be free to do so.

Lara listens attentively to her parents' conversation.

SPLATT'S HOUSE, IN THE LOUNGE, EVENING

Splatt's family is sitting around. The lounge, in contrast to Lara's, has things scattered everywhere. Lionel is fidgeting. Elaine sits quietly. Splatt just stares ahead. There's a knock at the door. Elaine gets up and answers the knock. Splatt is close enough to overhear the conversation, but Lionel is out of earshot.

> ELAINE
> Hello.

> MISS BARGE
> Are you Jonathan Drop's mother?

> ELAINE
> Yes, I am.

> MISS BARGE
> I'm Miss Barge, Jonathan's teacher.

> ELAINE
> I know who you are, we have met.

MISS BARGE
Yes, yes. Principal Schooner and I would like to meet with you and your husband as soon as possible. Would you be able to come to the school tomorrow?

Splatt hears this and cringes.

> ELAINE
> What is it in connection with, Miss Barge?

> MISS BARGE
> I think it will be better if you see for yourself the artwork that Jonathan has done on the greenboard.

> ELAINE
> Ok, tomorrow will be fine. Can we make it early?

> MISS BARGE
> Yes, any time after seven.

> ELAINE
> We'll see you tomorrow then.

She turns and slowly walks back into the lounge.

> LIONEL
> Who was that?

> ELAINE
> Jonathan's teacher. She wants to meet with us tomorrow.

Lionel jumps up in a rage and towers over Splatt.

LIONEL
I warned you, boy!

ELAINE
Lionel, stop! Jonathan isn't in trouble. Miss Barge just wants us to see his artwork.

Lionel slowly lowers his hand.

LIONEL
What art? Rebels don't do art, they just cause trouble.

ELAINE
Why are you so hard on Jonathan? This must be something special … the principal even wants to meet us.

She turns to Splatt.

ELAINE
I didn't know you were interested in the arts, sweetie.

Their eyes meet and Splatt can only muster an embarrassed smile.

SPLATT'S AND LARA'S BEDROOMS, EVENING

The camera alternates between shots of Splatt unable to sleep with eyes wide open, and Lara's eyes becoming heavy until finally she falls asleep.

Splatt, worried to death about what will happen the next day, gets out of bed and prepares to run away from home. On his way through the entrance hall, he knocks a shell ornament off the display. It crashes to the floor and breaks. He hides under the stairway with heart throbbing … When the coast is clear, he exits his home and proceeds down the road. He stops in front of Lara's home and tries to call to her.

OUTSIDE LARA'S HOUSE, EVENING

SPLATT
(whispering)
Lara … Lara!

Lara is fast asleep. Splatt ventures closer to her bedroom window and tries again.

SPLATT
Lara … Lara!

Still Lara is fast asleep. Splatt climbs up a seaweed creeper. He is balancing precariously. He calls again.

SPLATT
Lara, will you wake up … Lara!

Lara's eyes move but she does not wake up. Splatt, losing his balance, desperately tries one more time.

SPLATT
Lara!

Splatt loses his foothold and plunges to the seabed below. Lara's eyes are closed, but the thud of Splatt's fall wakes her. She opens her eyes. Splatt looks up at her dark window; he slowly turns and walks away with drooped shoulders. On the ground next to him, the light brightens, indicating that a light has been switched on behind him, but he does not notice. The camera pans to Lara's lit bedroom window. Splatt keeps slogging forward. The increased light on the ground next to him steadily fades until there is nothing left. Then Splatt hears the faintest whisper.

LARA
Splatt!

He turns and sees Lara's silhouette in her window. Splatt runs back and scrambles up the creeper.

LARA
What are you doing?

SPLATT
I don't have much time, Lara, and I am going to ask just one thing of you for now: *Trust me.* I'm in a whole lot of trouble at school and with my dad. I thought a lot about it tonight, and I can truthfully say that I don't think I did anything wrong. All I did was to go into the open ocean to get you some ink.

Lara smiles lovingly at him.

SPLATT

Then I got punished for that, but I did not write out my punishment. Instead, I fetched the ink where I had hidden it. I still wanted to give it to you—that's why I didn't dispose of it. And I wrote on the green-board in ink, "I must let go of the way I know," 'cause that's what the Color Drop told me, and—

LARA

(interrupting)

Strange you should say that. My mother, just tonight, said everyone is responsible for their own path—wherever it may lead.

SPLATT

Lara, just listen to me. So, Miss Barge came to my house because she wants to meet with my parents tomorrow, and I'm already in trouble with my dad for combing my hair. … Oh, don't worry. I asked that you trust me, and here's the thing—I don't expect you to come with me, but I really would like it. And I want you to know that I would have done this even if I wasn't in trouble. Maybe not tonight, but I would have. And if I wasn't in trouble, I would have had more time to explain things to you. But I am in trouble, and I'm leaving tonight to find the Land of Color. And I want you to come with me, and you will, if you trust me.

LARA
Phew, Splatt, this is sudden. I must admit, I gave it some thought—what you said today. But running away …

SPLATT
Lara, it's not running away—that's what I tried to tell you. Even if I wasn't in trouble, I would do this—the trouble just made my mind up sooner. I can't stay now. I have to go. … So, what will it be?

LARA
I need time.

SPLATT
I don't have time.

Splatt leans forward and kisses Lara goodbye.

SPLATT
Goodbye, Lara.

She doesn't reply. He looks into her eyes one last time, then climbs down and starts to walk away. The further away he is, the closer she is to tears. Then she collapses to the floor and sobs. She sobs for a while then gets up and peers out the window. In the distance, Splatt is just visible.

LARA
(whispering)
Splatt I … I trust you. Wait for me. I'm coming.

Lara frantically climbs through the window and down the creeper and sets out after Splatt. He is not visible anymore. She rushes through the village and when she gets to the perimeter where the open ocean starts, she scouts in all directions. Then she sees him in the far distance and starts running toward him.

> LARA
> *Splatt! Splatt, wait!*

At first, he doesn't hear her.

As Lara struggles forward, she is repeatedly lifted off her feet by the current. Each time it is worse. She looks forward and shouts desperately.

> LARA
> *Splatt!!*

Splatt now hears her. His face lights up, but as he turns, he sees the current sweep Lara off her feet and away from him. His joy turns to panic as he moves to rescue her, but as he takes one step forward, the current pushes him back two. He battles the current, but Lara is drifting further and further away from him. He grits his teeth and makes one last enormous effort forward, but the current picks him up as though he is a feather in the wind. As he is carried off, he screams.

> SPLATT
> *Lara, Lara!!!!*

When the vicious current subsides, Splatt lands on the bare ocean floor. It is virtually dark, and he is utterly alone. He peers out in all directions.

>SPLATT
>(shouting)
>*Lara! Where are you, Lara? Can you hear me?*

Silence.

>SPLATT
>(panicked)
>*Lara, can you hear me? Can anyone hear me? Lara!*

Silence. Splatt keeps on calling until he drops down with exhaustion and eventually falls asleep.

ON A YACHT ABOVE A TROPICAL REEF, DAWN

A diver—animated but human (BRET)—is underwater, pulling seaweed from an opening in the yacht's hull. He surfaces next to the yacht and climbs up the ladder at the back onto the deck. He unstraps his toolbelt, takes off his mask, and speaks to his girlfriend (SYLVIA).

BRET
All done, darling, it's fixed. We've got fresh water again.

SYLVIA
Was it seaweed blocking it?

BRET
Yep, totally clogged. I sometimes think it would be less hassle to cart fresh water along than to keep maintaining the desalination machine.

ON THE TROPICAL
REEF, DAWN

Painted on the side of the yacht is its name, *The Spirit of Freedom.* The camera retraces Bret's path back into the water, past the desalination opening in the hull—where many drops hover in a praying posture, and onto a beautiful coral reef with magnificently colored fish and coral. Under a coral sits Lara, looking forlorn but at the same time mesmerized by the array of color everywhere. A drop (REEF DROP) passes by.

LARA
Excuse me?

REEF DROP
(annoyed)
How many times must I tell you people, I'm not interested.

LARA
I'm sorry, I've been on an awful journey to land here—tossed, turned, and stretched by the currents. I just wanted to ask a question.

REEF DROP
Yeah, right. You think I don't know a Purist when I see one.

LARA
A Purist? I don't know what that is, but I'm not that. No, I'm a Sea Drop.

The Reef Drop comes closer and looks Lara up and down.

REEF DROP
Yeah right, you're a Sea Drop. Looks like just another trick of you Purists to convert me. I'm not interested. I'm a Reef Drop and will remain so.

LARA
(fascinated)
I've never met a Reef Drop or a Purist. I just wanted to ask if this is the Land of Color. You see, where I come from, everything is grey. I've never seen anything as beautiful as things are here. Surely this must be Colorland?

REEF DROP
Land of Color, Colorland—never heard of it. Actually, never heard of a Sea Drop either, so scram. Get out of here.

The Reef Drop menacingly looks at Lara, who retreats to where the Purists are hovering, not too far from the yacht's desalination entry. She calls to an elderly Purist woman (MARY).

LARA

Excuse me?

MARY

How, child, you've found your way to the fold.

LARA

No, no, you don't understand. I've lost my boyfriend, and I'm looking for the Land of Color. He'll be there. Can you help me?

MARY

Oh dear, you are blinded. See the waiting flock—we are the chosen ones. We are chosen to come out from amongst them and be separate. Behold, a miracle will occur when we are swept away to the Land of the Pure. Why bother with a Land of Color that will blind you to your true purpose.

ON A YACHT ABOVE A TROPICAL REEF, MORNING

Bret places a crate of empty mineral water bottles next to a sink.

> BRET
> (shouting over his shoulder)
> May as well make hay while the sun shines, darling.
> I'm filling all our empties with fresh water. Will you
> switch on for me?

> SYLVIA
> Sure, just a second.

Sylvia emerges from a cabin door and walks to an electrical switch with a large sign that reads "DESALINATOR ON/OFF." The switch is in the off position.

ON THE TROPICAL
REEF, MORNING

Mary takes Lara's hand.

MARY
Come child, you must join the fold.

LARA
Please, listen to me. Can you direct me to Colorland? I thought this might be it, but it can't be—my boyfriend is not here, and he knows to find me at Colorland.

ON A YACHT ABOVE A TROPICAL REEF, MORNING

Sylvia walks purposefully toward the switch.

ON THE TROPICAL REEF, MORNING

MARY
Child, I don't know of such a place, but it is clear that you are chosen. You have been led to us by grace. Stay here and you will be separated from those who conform.

ON A YACHT ABOVE A TROPICAL REEF, MORNING

Sylvia's hand reaches for the switch.

ON THE TROPICAL
REEF, MORNING

LARA
I think I'd rather go. I don't think you can help me.

ON A YACHT ABOVE A TROPICAL REEF, MORNING

Sylvia flicks the switch.

ON THE TROPICAL REEF, MORNING

As Lara starts moving away, the desalination machine huffs and puffs and then comes into full swing, creating a vortex that begins at the opening and spreads outward. It first sucks in the Purists that are closest, then those a little further away, and eventually Mary who was at the edge is sucked in. It appears Lara will escape this fate, but the suction vortex inches closer to where she is now—desperately trying to outrun it. Lara is failing and is slowly reeled in. When she reaches the edge of the funnel, she manages to get hold of and cling to the edge. But the suction is strong. Her arms and legs start to stretch; her little body becomes elongated until finally she can hold on no longer.

LARA
(screaming)
No! No!

She is rushed through the funnel toward a paper filter. Her body is squashed and squeezed through the filter. She screams in agony. Then she's dragged toward a charcoal filter where the process is repeated. With every filtering, her body becomes paler.

IN A WATER
BOTTLE, MORNING

Lara emerges from the tap and lands in a blue plastic bottle. Above her, the cap is screwed on by a human hand to seal her fate. The bottle is then placed in a yellow crate next to others.

> LARA
> (banging her fists on the bottle)
> *Let me out! Let me out, I tell you!*

She starts to cry.

> LARA
> (sobbing softly)
> Let me out. Please, let me out.

She sinks to the bottom, where she lies in a fetal position, crying.

BARE OCEAN FLOOR, MORNING

Splatt wakes up. He stretches and rubs his eyes. Then he realizes where he is.

> SPLATT
> (to himself)
> Lara? Color? *Oh no, man. No!*

Two stern-looking drops (DEEP DROP 1 and DEEP DROP 2) approach. They are vigilante border patrollers.

> DEEP DROP 1
> You want to show me some ID, kid?

> SPLATT
> (with shaky voice)
> ID, what's that?

> DEEP DROP 1
> (to Splatt)
> Don't fool around with me, kid. You illegals are all the same—pretending you know nothing.

DEEP DROP 1
(to Deep Drop 2, laughing sarcastically)
At least this one speaks English.

DEEP DROP 1
(to Splatt)
So, what's the story here? You're a decoy so your whole family can cross the border elsewhere? And of course, you know you'll be deported and then you'll sneak back in later. So, what's your story, kid? And don't lie to me.

SPLATT
My story? Hey, man, I'm lost. I was looking for—

DEEP DROP 1
You don't "Hey, man" me, kid.

SPLATT
(realizing he's in trouble)
Sorry, sir, but I don't know what "deport" is.

DEEP DROP 1
I don't know where you're from, but deporting means you're going back to where you came from. We send you back home. This land is *our* land. My forefathers fought for this land, and we intend to keep it for ourselves. We don't need any more foreigners taking our jobs, taking over our land, and marrying our daughters. Here we pay respect one to another. You … you people can't organize your own territories, and then

you want come share in the wealth that we've created. Oh no, sonny boy, not as long as I can patrol this border. I'll keep you no-goods out if it's the last thing I do. It's because so many of you illegals are trying to steal what belongs to us that the government is unable to patrol this border properly. But you no-goods didn't reckon that us citizens of Deep Drop Land would pull together to nail your little butts, did you now?

DEEP DROP 2
(to Deep Drop 1)
Come on, mate, He's just a kid.

SPLATT
That's right … um, sir. I was just looking for a place—Colorland, when … when a current swept me away and landed me here.

DEEP DROP 1
(to Splatt)
Nonsense! Never heard such a load of bollocks in my life.

DEEP DROP 2
(to Deep Drop 1)
What if he's telling the truth?

DEEP DROP 1
Don't you go soft on me now! I don't believe a word of it. I'm going to fetch the immigration officials. You

look after the no-good and keep your eyes peeled for his family trying to cross.

Deep Drop 1 turns and disappears into the distance.

SPLATT
Sir?

DEEP DROP 2
Yes?

SPLATT
Sir, I'm pleading with you. Sir, please believe me. Sir, you can't send me back home. Please, sir.

Deep Drop 2 pretends not to be listening.

SPLATT
Sir, I cannot be deported … Actually, sir, I'm in big trouble at home … I don't think I should be in big trouble for what I did, but they think I should. That's why … that's why I ran away from home. No, actually, that's not why I ran away from home. I really ran away because I wanted to find Colorland, but that's not why I can't be deported. I can't be deported because my girlfriend followed me, and we got separated by the current. And I know—no, I think I know—that she knows that I think she will not stop until she finds Colorland. Because she thinks that I think that she thinks that, and that is the reason why I have to find Colorland—to find her, because she

thinks I won't go back. And I think she won't go back to Sea Drop High, and that's why the only way to find her is to find Colorland.

DEEP DROP 2
Did you say Sea Drop High?

SPLATT
Yes, sir, that's where we ran away from.

Deep Drop 2 scratches his chin and thinks for a while.

SPLATT
You have to believe me, sir.

DEEP DROP 2
Shush, I'm thinking.

Then after a while, Deep Drop 2's face lights up as though he has found the answer.

DEEP DROP 2
Look, if you hadn't said you were a Sea Drop, I would have kept you here. But Sea Drops, as much as I disagree with their Thunder God, don't ever try and enter Deep Drop Land illegally. And it's really my duty to keep you here and deport you 'cause you're still a minor. But considering how oppressive your society is, I'm gonna let you go, and I'll think of an excuse for why you escaped. So, get the hell out of here.

Splatt immediately scoots off.

DEEP DROP 2

Not in that direction, fool. That's straight into Deep Drop Land. This way. The border is not too far, and once you've crossed it, no one can touch you—so run.

Deep Drop 2 points in the direction Splatt must run, and when Splatt is some distance away, calls after him.

DEEP DROP 2

And kid, be careful... (then he whispers) ... and forget about the Colorland—it doesn't exist.

As Splatt disappears in the far distance, Deep Drop 1 arrives back.

DEEP DROP 2

You were right, mate, the little trickster. I turned my back for only a moment, and he vanished into the wide ocean. I say we track the border to find his illegal family.

LARA'S HOUSE, MORNING

Catharine walks towards Lara's bedroom. She recites her morning wake-up call.

CATHARINE
Get up, get up, get out of the bed. Come, sweetie.

She pushes the half-open door fully open and sees the empty bed.

CATHARINE
Len! Len!

LEN
Yes, darling?

CATHARINE
Come quickly, Lara's gone!

Len rushes up the stairs, shouting.

LEN
What do you mean, gone?

Len appears and sees the empty bed.

LEN
Good gracious, no.

Len and Catharine look at each other.

CATHARINE
Splatt … the Land of Color… No, it can't be!

LEN
I'll go to Splatt's house.

He rushes over to Splatt's house. Lionel answers the door.

LEN
Morning. Are you Splatt's father?

LIONEL
(annoyed)
There's no Splatt in this house, only a Jonathan.

LEN
(anxious)
Look—Splatt, Jonathan, what does it matter? Is he home?

LIONEL
The little brat's still sleeping. Why?

LEN
I'm Lara's father, and she's not at home this morning. Her bed has been slept in, but she's gone. I fear—

LIONEL
(interrupting)
The little rebel, let me check. If he's got anything to do with this, I'll teach him a lesson proper. Hold here, let me check.

Lionel turns and walks a distance away then shouts upstairs.

LIONEL
Elaine! Check if your brat's in his room. I got Lara's pa here—she's missing. (then to himself) As sure as Thunder God, I'll teach him proper.

Elaine checks Splatt's bedroom and sees he's not there. She dashes down the stairs to the front door, where Lionel has returned to.

ELAINE
(to Len)
Good morning, I'm Elaine, Jonathan's mother.

LEN
Morning. Our daughter is missing, I was just wondering if your son—

ELAINE
Jonathan is also not here, but his teacher, Miss Barge, came by last night and wanted to meet with my husband and me this morning to discuss some artwork he had done. I guess he must have gone to school early because of this excitement. My husband and I

are leaving shortly to meet with Miss Barge and the principal. Maybe you would also like to come down there. I'm sure it will all be OK.

LEN
I'm not so sure. You see, Lara was asking about a Land of Color last night, and … Oh, it doesn't matter. Let's get down to the school right now. We'll see you there shortly.

Elaine closes the door behind Len.

LIONEL
(to Elaine)
What's Johnathan's story with the Land of Color? I'll knock the rebel thinking right out of him.

ELAINE
Come quickly. Let's get down to the school.

LIONEL
Now?

Elaine grabs Lionel by the hand.

ELAINE
Come, we must go right now.

CLASSROOM, MORNING

Miss Barge and Principal Schooner are waiting for Splatt's parents to arrive. Both sets of parents arrive at the same time. They walk in and see Splatt's "artwork" on the greenboard. Lionel immediately jumps the gun.

LIONEL
(furious)
The little rebel brat. See, now? See, Elaine, what your son has been up to?

PRINCIPAL SCHOONER
This cannot be tolerated. We must take serious action—

ELAINE
Wait. Wait! Has anyone seen our children?

LEN
No, that's why we're here. Lara is missing.

PRINCIPAL SCHOONER
Yes, yes, that can wait. The matter at hand is what you see on the greenboard in front of you.

ELAINE
(to Principal Schooner)
Our children are missing, and all you can think of is what punishment to dish out. What's with you people, have you lost all your senses?

LIONEL
Elaine, quiet before you start annoying me.

ELAINE
No, Lionel, I've kept my mouth shut for too many years. No more! I'm speaking now. Our children are missing, don't you understand?

PRINCIPAL SCHOONER
I'm sure they'll turn up sooner or later, but we must address this insubordination now.

ELAINE
(to Principal Schooner)
Are you out of your mind? Can you not see the obvious? Jonathan has run away because he couldn't bear what you might dish out, and he's taken Lara with him. Yes, you all are out of your mind. It's precisely this strict, unbending dogma that is preached here in this school and in homes like ours that would make kids rebel and … and … and run away from home. You people, you're so obsessed with your dogma that you fail to see the real issue at hand. Our kids are missing!

Lara's parents Len and Catharine are dumfounded, almost in shock at what's unfolding.

LIONEL
(very serious)
Elaine, you're really annoying me now. I'll, I'll—

ELAINE
(interrupting)
You'll what, Lionel? I'm speaking now, and you will all listen. Our children are missing. I hold you responsible (she points at Miss Barge), and you (she points at Principal Schooner) and *you* (she points at Lionel)!

PRINCIPAL SCHOONER
You have no right—

ELAINE
(interrupting)
No right? I *do* have a right. You all know that our school's constitution states that any parent may run to be a teacher in any subject, and that by a majority vote of parents such person *will be* appointed so.

PRINCIPAL SCHOONER
That's never been done and never will be.

ELAINE
Oh, yes? I'll show you that it will be. I'll call a Parent Teacher Association meeting, and I'll tell the parents

that they too may lose their children. And I know, 'cause I'm a mother, that no self-respecting parent would stand by your stupid rules and regulations if they knew they could lose a child. And I'll take over this school, and I'll change the curriculum … and … and I'll change everything that I have kept my mouth shut about for too many years.

LIONEL
Elaine, you've lost your mind.

ELAINE
No, Lionel, I have never been clearer. Let's put it to the test then. Let's do this right now: We are four parents here—let's vote. Let's vote right now. All in favor of the Sea Drop dogma, show your hands.

Lionel, Miss Barge, and Principal Schooner raise their hands.

ELAINE
(pointing at Miss Barge and Principal Schooner)
Not you two, you're not parents. So, that's one vote for you people. And now, all in favor of my proposal, show your hands.

Elaine, Len, and Catharine raise their hands.

ELAINE
See? There you have it.

LIONEL
You're on your own, Elaine.

ELAINE
Yes, Lionel, I've been on my own for a long time.
(then to Len and Catharine) I'm so sorry that you
had to witness this, but my sole purpose is to find my
child, and if I do, I don't want him to be subjected
to this … this … lunacy that made him run away in
the first place.

LIONEL
I should have known where the little brat got his
rebel genes from. I see it clearly now. I want you out
of my house.

ELAINE
You want me out of your house? I'd sooner be on the
street than go back to *your house*. My only regret is
that I didn't stand up for myself sooner. It's not me
that's on my own Lionel—it's you.

CATHARINE
(to Elaine)
You can stay with us in the meantime—right, Len?

LEN
Of course.

CATHARINE

That way we can put our heads together to try and find them. *Oh, no!*

Catharine breaks into tears and sobs on Len's shoulder.

CATHARINE

Will we ever see dearest sweetest Lara again? Oh, no!

IN A WATER BOTTLE, AFTERNOON

Lara's panic and anger has subsided. Mary comes over to her.

MARY
Feeling better now, dear?

LARA
Not really.

Mary introduces herself.

MARY
I'm Mary. What's your name, child?

LARA
Lara.

MARY
You may not know this yet, Lara, but you are one of the chosen few. You have been redeemed and purified.

LARA

No, I haven't. All that has happened is that the salt has been sucked from my system against my own will.

MARY

In time you will realize the miracle that you have been chosen to be part of. Why don't you become quiet at your core, as the rest of us are, and you will soon be thankful for your redemption?

LARA

Did you not hear what I said? I don't want to be trapped here. I want to find Colorland—that's where my boyfriend will be. I need to get out.

MARY

Dearie, you are in the Land of the Pure. Why resist the miracle? Why don't you just try to become quiet, and soon you will realize …

Lara is frustrated; she rolls her eyes back and does not answer.

BARE OCEAN
FLOOR, AFTERNOON

Splatt is struggling forward. He's visibly weary. From the light growing stronger and the uphill gradient that he is facing, it is clear that he is moving away from the deep sea and into shallower water. A single plankton drifts past him, then a pair, but he does not notice. Increasingly more plankton float by until plankton surround him everywhere. He now takes notice of these strange little creatures.

Then an enormous basking shark (a plankton-eating shark) appears in the distance. Splatt does not notice the shark; he is preoccupied with the plankton. The shark gets closer and closer. As water enters its mouth, it is plankton rich, but the water that exits from its gills is plankton free.

The shark passes overhead; its shadow darkens the entire ocean floor around Splatt. The current that the shark's tail creates is powerful; it lifts Splatt from the ocean floor and jerks him about in all directions. Then the shark turns abruptly and heads straight for where Splatt is.

Splatt sees the shark coming and desperately tries to get out of the way, but in vain. He travels straight into the mouth of the shark. Disoriented, he screams as he summersaults toward the gill rakers—a fine mesh-like substance that serves as a strainer to remove the plankton. Splatt is forced through a tiny square in the mesh, head and arms first. Then he gets stuck with half of his body out and the other half in. The gill rakers then contract, enabling the shark to swallow its catch of plankton. This threatens to tear Splatt in half.

Splatt feverishly uses his arms to worm the rest of his body through the tiny hole in the mesh where he had become stuck—and just in time. He is expelled with the plankton-free water. Exhausted and very relieved, he floats down to the ocean floor, and the further he goes, the more an expression of excitement lights his face. When he lands, he raises his fist in victory and exclaims,

> SPLATT
> It was all a lie. I'm alive. *I'm alive!*

Then he notices the same Color Drop that he had seen before, lying to his left—again, with both hands cupped behind his head and his thin legs crossed. Except this time, the drop is yellow (YELLOW DROP).

> SPLATT
> Hey. What color are you this time?

> YELLOW DROP
> Yellow.

SPLATT
I like yellow, too. Hey, you've got to help me here.

YELLOW DROP
With what?

SPLATT
I don't believe you, "With what"—with finding Colorland! It's really important now. I have to find Lara.

YELLOW DROP
I told you: you need to find your own way.

SPLATT
Don't start with that—it's because of you that I'm in this mess, and now you won't help me.

YELLOW DROP
Because of me? Didn't you tell Lara you would have gone in search of the Land of Color even if you weren't in trouble?

SPLATT
Yeah, but … wait a minute … how do you know what I told Lara?

YELLOW DROP
I know a lot of things.

SPLATT
(amazed)

You do? So, then you must know how important it is
to me to find Lara?

YELLOW DROP
Yep.

SPLATT
Then why won't you help me find Colorland?

YELLOW DROP
I told you already: you need to find your own way.

SPLATT
How?

YELLOW DROP
Maybe you should continue to let go more of the way
you know.

SPLATT
I did, I even got swallowed by a giant fish—and I
survived. What more must I let go of?

YELLOW DROP
That's for you to work out.

With that, the yellow drop disappears as quickly as he came.

IN A WATER
BOTTLE, EVENING

All the Purist Drops are asleep, but not Lara. Her eyes are heavy, but she forces herself to stay awake. The camera zooms into one of Lara's eyes, then fades to reveal her thoughts. She sees Splatt in the schoolyard telling his friends how he punched the Ink Fish right in the ink gland. Fading brings the shot back from the playground to Lara's face. She smiles, then her eyes close and she sleeps.

BARE OCEAN FLOOR, EVENING

Splatt is also falling asleep. (The camera similarly zooms into Splatt's right eye. He sees himself outside Lara's widow saying, "I don't have much time, Lara, and I am going to ask just one thing of you for now: *Trust me.*" Then he sees how the current separates them. A single tear rolls down his cheek before his eyes close and he falls asleep.

SCHOOL HALL, EVENING

The school hall is packed with parents. On the stage are two podiums; Elaine is at one, and Miss Barge and Principal Schooner at the other. Behind Principal Schooner is what seems to be a greenboard covered with a woven seaweed cloth. Principal Schooner addresses the audience.

PRINCIPAL SCHOONER
Good evening parents, and a hearty welcome to Sea Drop High tonight. As you are aware, Jonathan Drop and Lara Drop have absconded from our fine society.

ELAINE
Not absconded, more like were forced to run away.

PRINCIPAL SCHOONER
(to Elaine)
Please, madam, you will have your chance, and I will have the good manners not to interrupt you. You see, parents, this is just one small example of how a society without strict rules and regulations can collapse into anarchy. Now, as I was saying, they absconded from our fine society—why? This is what each one of us has to ask of ourselves: why? I'll tell you why. Jonathan Drop—or Splatt as he prefers to be

called—forsook his righteous heritage, took it upon himself to venture into the open ocean to find ink—from an Ink Fish—purely to impress Lara Drop with his rebelliousness. Miss Barge, being the fine tutor that she is, discovered this and ordered him to dispose of the ink. He disobeyed her explicit instruction to dispose of the ink and must have hidden it somewhere. His punishment for venturing outside of our safe enclave was to write out—a mere three hundred times, I would have you know—that he would not venture into the open ocean again. But what did he do instead?

Principal Schooner turns and with one sweep removes the cloth to reveal Splatt's artwork.

PRINCIPAL SCHOONER

This, dear parents, is what Jonathan Drop did with the ink he was supposed to dispose of. Defiant? I'd say. Insubordinate? Most definitely. A cancer amongst our youth? I say "yes." Sea Drop High has a long tradition: through discipline we mold worthy adult Sea Drops, but this one I think was beyond redemption. You see, he not only defied all rules by venturing into the open ocean—and we all know how dangerous that is—he also showed no remorse when he was caught, as you can clearly see from what he did. Instead of gracefully accepting his punishment, he gave us this. (He points to the greenboard.) But … and wait for this, because this is beyond my comprehension—all of the above pales when considering what he did next.… He then is such a coward that he ran away and … he coerced one of our most outstanding pupils to go with him. I think these despicable acts should be severely punished—that's if he ever makes it back here. Now this woman (he points to Elaine) wants to take over this fine establishment and liberalize it and breed more of the cancer that Jonathan Drop is. When you are asked to vote, dear parents, I ask only one thing of you: be true to your essence. We are, after all, Sea Drops with a proud heritage. I thank you.

Throughout Principal Schooner's speech, Elaine almost loses her cool several times, but she manages to bite her lip and stick it out to the end. She takes the podium.

ELAINE
Good evening parents, moms and dads. Does this ring a bell? Junior is in trouble. He's hurt himself. He calls, "Mommy, Daddy!" You've all heard it, and, boy, do we rush when our child is hurt! But that's not all, there's "Mommy, why this?" and "Daddy, why that?" And all to too soon they become teenagers and then young adults, but to us they always remain our children.

We love to help, to teach, and to guide, and none of us want what's bad for our children. So, we teach, and we instruct, and we mold—all with one goal: that our children can be as great as they possibly can. Not forgetting the "Good night, Mommy, good night, Daddy." We love them. We love them in the morning, at noon when they come home from school with their stories of the day, and at night when they go to sleep. And we're amazed how quickly the time has passed since the days when we used to put them to bed and they said "Night, Mommy." And even though they now say, "Night, Mom," we remember the "Good night, Mommy."

We also love them when they're naughty. Yes, we do, and then we have to decide how to deal with it—will we mete out judgment that will ruin their self-esteem, like calling them a cancer? Cancer, ladies and gentlemen, is when bad cells force good cells to become cancerous until the entire body dies. Principal Schooner called my child a cancer—he obviously has never heard my Jonathan say "Good night, Mommy." (Her voice cracks, and she has to take a while to regain her composure.)

Cancer? My child is not a cancer. What does he stand accused of? Do you know? He is accused of that which is in all of us and defines our very nature— curiosity, ladies and gentlemen, curiosity. My child has the sweetest nature. He is intelligent, sensitive, and yes, he is curious.

Who said going into the open ocean is wrong? I ask of you, who was the first to say this? Anybody?

Anybody? We just accept that somewhere in some stupid code of conduct of Sea Drops, it is legislated that this is so. And no one, none of us have had the courage to ask, "Why not?" We just accepted it. Is that who we are as a society? Do we, and do we have to, just accept?

But there was one that had an inquiring mind. One individual that stood above the rest of us that just accepts. This individual had the courage not only to explore, but to bring back proof. Proof to whom? I'll tell you: to his girlfriend, whom he esteems very highly.

I ask this of you, ladies and gentlemen, if my son thought he had committed such a terrible sin, would he have flaunted this in front of his sweetheart? I say no. Jonathan stands accused of being inquisitive. It is the rules that are adhered to in this school—rules none of us know where they come from or even possibly why they exist—that judge my son to have committed this infringement. But no one can tell me why it is so wrong. Did he hurt anyone by doing it? Did he take from another that which did not belong to him? How did his actions affect anyone except for Miss Barge and Principal Schooner, who at all costs want to enforce these rules and take it personally if anyone dares go beyond their boundaries? And for that you call my son a cancer—shame on you!

So, ladies and gentlemen, in conclusion: If you vote for me, you vote for change. You vote for someone who will ask, "Why is this rule in place?" And if there is no good reason, let's scrap it. Not someone who tries to enforce stupid rules in such a brutal way that my Jonathan had no choice but to run away. When you vote, ask yourselves: would I want to lose those beautiful sounds— "Mommy" and "Daddy"—to a stupid rule like I did? And if you vote for me, you won't. I thank you all.

The vote takes place, and Elaine wins by an overwhelming majority. Lionel is indecisive but in the end votes against Elaine. Principal Schooner and Miss Barge leave the stage defeated and walk out the back.

PRINCIPAL SCHOONER
(to Miss Barge)
Give that woman enough rope and she'll hang herself. You just watch.

MISS BARGE
I'm not so sure. I must tell you that somehow, she struck a chord deep inside of me.

PRINCIPAL SCHOONER
You're not going soft on me as well, are you?

MISS BARGE
Of course not, I was just saying.

PRINCIPAL SCHOONER
Don't let the evil beguile you, Miss Barge. She is darkness masquerading as light. You just wait and see.

Back on stage, Elaine thanks the audience.

ELAINE
Thank you, thank you.

THE ARCH AT THE ENTRANCE
TO THE SCHOOL, MORNING

An adult Sea Drop is chalking-writing new designations to the school's sign.

SEA DROP HIGH SCHOOL
Principal—Mrs. Elaine
Sea Drop Orientation—Mrs. Elaine
Religious Instruction—Mrs. Elaine

BARE OCEAN
FLOOR, MORNING

Splatt wakes up. A short distance behind him, a sand shelf is visible, indicating that he is close to land. Splatt climbs up the shelf, heaving. When he reaches the top, a whole new world unfolds before his eyes. Hundreds of little drops with dreadlocks are slowly bopping up and down with the movement of the waves. Splatt swims up and closer to investigate the happenings. A Surf Drop (SEAN) calls out to him.

> SEAN
> (above the roar of the waves)
> Hey, dude, careful there, you'll break the surface, like, and then you're a goner.

> SPLATT
> (still rising toward the surface)
> What's that? I can't hear you.

Splatt, having never been close to the surface and not knowing what it looks like, is unaware that he's approaching the surface rapidly. Sean lunges upward and catches Splatt by the leg just before he reaches the surface and pulls him down.

SEAN
Like, what's up, dude, have you lost your pip or what?

SPLATT
My what?

SEAN
Where you from, dude? Like, the first thing you need to learn if you wanna go surfing is to avoid the surface. If I didn't catch you, you'd have been tickets, dude.

SPLATT
(smiling sheepishly)
Sorry, I was warned about the surface, but I'm a Sea Drop. We never come close to the surface. Actually, I've never seen the surface before.

Sean laughs and sticks his hand out.

SEAN
I'm Sean.

Splatt tries to shake Sean's hand in the usual fashion, but Sean forces a handshake that goes from normal to upside down and then back to normal again.

SPLATT
(unsure of himself)
Hi, I'm Splatt.

SEAN
So, what brings you to our sunshine coast, dude?

SPLATT

That's a long story, but basically, I'm looking for a place—Colorland.

SEAN

(rubbing his dreadlocks out of his face and pondering a while)

I think I know what you're looking for, dude, but it's dangerous. Have you surfed before?

SPLATT

Surfed? I don't know what that is, "surf?"

SEAN

Oh, oh. I think you got a problem.

SPLATT

What? Why? Hey, this is important to me, like, very important. You don't understand.

SEAN

OK, dude, like we say: anything for the brotherhood. But you'll have to learn to surf.

SPLATT

Anything, man.

SEAN

Sure?

SPLATT
Yes, I'm sure. So, can you please explain what surfing is and how it will get me to Colorland?

SEAN
OK. Surfing is dangerous. Why is it dangerous? Because if you get it wrong, you can either evaporate on the surface, which means death, or—and this is important and where the whole glitch comes in with Colorland.

SPLATT
What glitch?

SEAN
You really know nothing, hey, dude? Surfing is catching a wave that's on its way to the beach. If you're too high on the wave, you might evaporate. And hey, I don't have to tell you what that means. If you ride the wave too far, you'll end up on the beach. And then there's no way back, and sure as surfing is the greatest thing ever, you gonna evaporate on the beach, dude. Problem now is this Colorland you're looking for—it's sort of a Catch-22. See, when you're surfing you can see all these colors on the beach. I believe they're called sunbrellas or something like that. Humans like to sit under them. Problem is, you can't get there, 'cause if you beach, you're dead, dude, and I mean dead. So, see, you can see the Colorland when you're surfing, but you can't go there.

SPLATT
I'll take my chances. When do we start?

SEAN
We can do it right now.

SPLATT
Ok, so let's go.

SEAN
Not so fast, dude. There's a whole lot of stuff I gotta teach you before we go, but first—what's with that hairstyle of yours? It's so uncool. If you wanna hang with Surf Drops, I think you should—

SPLATT
(interrupting)
Hey, who cares about a hairstyle? I got more important things to do than worry about my hair. Now, will you teach me?

SEAN
Cool it, dude, I didn't mean to ruffle you.

SPLATT
Sure. So, can we start?

SEAN
Yeah, why not? And who cares about a hairstyle anyway? So, the first thing you need to know, and this is super important, dude: stay away from the surface.

You need to hang lowish to wait for a wave. And when the right one comes, you swim like all hell with the wave, then it breaks. Cool, this is when surfing starts. I even get goosed just thinking about it, dude.

SPLATT
Yes, yes, but then what?

SEAN
OK, so what you have to do is this—and this is even more super important: you stay at the bottom of the surf. Surf is like water that's rough and bubbles a lot. Now, you gotta make sure there's surf above you, else you stand a chance that the big E hits you, you know, evaporation. Dude, if the big E hits you, you're gone—gone forever. You see, dude, that's what makes surfing so cool, 'cause it's so dangerous. Man, you gotta experience it, you gotta feel it to know what—

SPLATT
Come on now, Sean, m...a...n. I just want to get to the Colorland. Help me here.

SEAN
Sorry, dude, I just get carried away 'cause it's so awesome. But I check where you at and ... the next thing, well this is the most super important of all that I've told you. Listen carefully—this might just save your life: *Rather U too soon than too late.*

SPLATT

"U," what is "U?"

SEAN

U, dude, is to make a U-ie. The wave will continue onto the beach—that's sure death. So, to U, you gotta dive down and let the wave roll over you. If you leave it too late, you can't dive down because there's no water underneath the wave, and then the wave is gonna carry you onto the beach, dude. And the rest, no, not the rest—actually you are history. You get it?

SPLATT

Yeah, I get it, but when do I see Colorland?

SEAN

As you're surfing forward, dude. You can't miss it, but the thrill is riding the wave.

SPLATT

So, can we go now?

SEAN

Sure, but listen, surfing is dangerous, way dangerous. So, I'll be next to you all the way. First, we'll do short practice runs until you have the hang of it. When I shout "U-ie," you duck down for all you're worth, see, dude?

SPLATT

Sure.

SEAN
Now, the right way to do it once you've caught the wave is to have your right arm outstretched in front of you and your left arm next to your side.

Sean demonstrates the posture. Splatt awkwardly imitates.

SEAN
So, for your first run, dude, just remember: if you do catch a wave—which I doubt you will, not on a first run, but if you do—stay at the bottom of the surf. And when I shout "U-ie," you duck down. Ready?

SPLATT
Ready.

Splatt and Sean swim closer to the surface where waves are noticeable. They hang in the water waiting for a wave. When it comes, Sean shouts.

SEAN
Swim! Swim, dude! Faster! Harder!

Splatt, with a look of utter determination, swims for all he's worth. The wave breaks. Sean surfs perfectly next to Splatt, who is tumbling head over heels. Splatt, with closed eyes, grits his teeth and assumes the right-arm-out position. This stabilizes him, and soon he's surfing next to Sean, albeit not nearly as skillfully.

SEAN
(shouting above the roar)
Hey, dude, isn't this ultracool?

Splatt is not listening to him. He is too busy scouting for Colorland ahead. And then he sees it: a myriad of colors on the beach. His face lights up. Now he has an even more determined look on his face, and his right arm is pointing to where he's going.

SEAN
U-ie, dude. (then louder) U-ie, dude! (then panicked)
Hey dude, U-ie now!!!

Splatt looks at him, acknowledging that he heard him, but makes no attempt to dive down.

SEAN
(in a last-ditch attempt)
U-ie NOW!!!!

Then for his own preservation, Sean ducks down, and Splatt rides the wave out onto the beach. As the wave retreats, Splatt is left on the sand. Slowly he starts sinking into the sand. He uses his hands and arms in attempt to slow the sinking but in vain; he is sinking fast. His body disappears under the sand until only two little hands are visible, desperately clinging on.

The camera pans to the next approaching wave as it rolls shoreward. All hopes are now pinned on this wave to save

Splatt. But one of his hands can hold on no longer, and it loses grip.

As the only remaining hand starts unclenching, mercifully, the wave arrives. Now Splatt's second hand becomes visible again, and slowly he emerges. But he has little time because the wave is retreating again. Splatt manages to get a few yards closer to the ocean before he is left on the sand again. Now he only sinks in halfway before the next wave arrives.

Two more waves and he's back in the ocean. He makes his way to where the surfers hang out. When Sean spots Splatt approaching, he points, suggesting that Splatt is the one he's been telling them about. Splatt gets a hero's welcome.

> SEAN
> Dude, I can't believe it, you're alive. You're the man, man. How'd ya do it?

All the surfers eagerly await Splatt's story.

> SPLATT
> It was nothing, really. I just wanted to get to where the color was. And hey, Sean, you were right … and also you were wrong—

> SEAN
> Cool, I was right … (softly) and I was wrong. (then excited) Yeah, of course I was wrong. I told you you're gone if you beach, and check here you are, dude.

SPLATT

No, Sean. You were right that no one could get there—to where the colors are. And you were wrong, dead wrong that it was Colorland. How can it be, if no drop can get there? Then it might as well not exist.

ONE OF THE SURFERS

What you on about, dude? You've just done what none of us ever had the guts to do. That must be the ultimate rush, dude—like to stare death in the face. What's it like, dude, awesome, hey?

SPLATT

No, not really. Fact is, I was petrified.

SURFERS IN UNISON

Awesome, dude.

SPLATT

You guys don't understand.

Splatt looks to Sean for support, but Sean understands as little as the rest.

SEAN

You are the man, man! So, can you teach us?

SPLATT

Sorry, guys, I have to go. I don't have time.

SEAN

You can't go, dude, you're a legend! Wait till the chicks hear about your bravery, you could pull the best, man. Why don't you wanna hang here? Come on, dude!

SPLATT

You never did hear a word I said, did you, Sean? Again and again, I tried to tell you something that's important to me, but you just didn't listen. Thanks for the lesson, but I've got to go.

SEAN

Where to, dude? You're in paradise here.

SPLATT

It doesn't matter.

BARE OCEAN
FLOOR, AFTERNOON

Splatt has left the Surf Drops behind and is forging forward in shallow water close to the shore. Then the Color Drop appears—same as before—except this time he is green (GREEN DROP).

SPLATT
And this time?

GREEN DROP
Green.

SPLATT
Nice one.

GREEN DROP
What do you mean?

SPLATT
I nearly got myself killed because I listened to you. You said that I should let go of the way I know even more, and I risked it and nearly got myself killed.

GREEN DROP

It seems you weren't listening. I told you all along that you have to find your own way, and that to find this way you'd have to let go of the way you know. Is that reason to blame me for the decisions you make? And besides, who said it was a wrong decision? Maybe, just maybe, it's another step in finding your way to Colorland. You are still going there?

SPLATT

Of course, I am. How else will I find Lara?

GREEN DROP

Only you know the way.

SPLATT

No, it's because of you that I've landed here.

GREEN DROP

You don't listen. It's because of *you* that you're here. I didn't tell you to do anything. I simply told you to find your own way by letting go of the way you know.

SPLATT

OK, OK, but are you going to help me?

GREEN DROP

I have been.

SPLATT

Then, where is it, Colorland?

GREEN DROP
How many times must I tell you, you need to find your own way?

SPLATT
That's not helping me at all!

GREEN DROP
Yes, it is.

SPLATT
How?

GREEN DROP
I'll tell you: you need to let go of more.

With that, the green drop disappears.

SPLATT
Come back here you … you! You told me nothing.

The green drop reappears.

GREEN DROP
It's only because of what I told you that you have come this far.

The green drop disappears again.

SPLATT
Come back here, I tell you, come back!

Splatt's calling out is in vain. It is almost dark by now, and Splatt collapses and falls asleep on the sand. … The following morning when it gets light, Splatt stretches and rubs his eyes.

IN A WATER BOTTLE, AFTERNOON

Lara stares blankly ahead. Her face is expressionless. She looks as though she doesn't care anymore. Mary approaches.

> MARY
> You've been sitting like this all morning, sweetie, staring at nothing. What's going on?

Lara does not answer. She keeps staring blankly ahead of her.

> MARY
> Not feeling well then, dear? You're becoming worse by the day. We must do something about this. Ah, I know what'll just be the ticket. Yes, yes.

Lara still just stares blankly.

> MARY
> Why don't you join us in our afternoon prayer, dear? I promise it'll make you feel a whole lot better. It will give you hope. Come on, dearie.

Mary offers a hand, and Lara doesn't resist. As they walk off though, Lara gets a hold of herself and starts pulling back.

LARA
I know you mean well, but I'd rather not.

MARY
When you're ready, sweetie, when you're ready.

Lara comes back to where she had been before, sits down, and stares blankly ahead.

LARA'S HOUSE, IN THE LOUNGE, AFTERNOON

Elaine arrives at Lara's house after her first day of teaching. She finds Len and Catharine in the lounge.

ELAINE
What a day. It was a nightmare!

CATHARINE
Nightmare?

ELAINE
Yes. All I could think of all day is where our children might be. And there I was with all these children, and I had no idea what to teach them. It was so horrendous. I started by going through all the Sea Drop rules one by one, and I asked the class why these rules were in place—because if there was no good reason, we should scrap them. But each time, neither the class nor I could find a reason to keep or discard them. It led to confusion, and oh my word, what a disaster. But that wasn't the worst: when I said we should investigate our belief in Thunder God, I came up against a brick wall, 'cause none of us knew

123

how to approach this. I can just imagine what they're going to tell their parents tonight. And all the time at the back of my mind was Jonathan and Lara. There must be something we can do to find them.

Elaine takes a deep breath. Len and Catharine listen intently.

CATHARINE
You're not suggesting we go searching in the ocean?

ELAINE
On my way home, I gave that very idea some thought. I was thinking, what's my priority here, educating others' children or finding my own? And that we have the support of other parents for now. And this was my idea: We must call for volunteers who will form a search party. Then we go into the ocean—bit-by-bit, and further and further, to see if we can find any clue as to where they might be. But against my own teachings of the day, I got scared—scared of the ocean—and I canned the idea.

LEN
That's exactly it. Why don't we do it? We can go out cautiously one step at a time. And we will learn—and not only will we learn, you can then impart to your class what we have learned.

CATHARINE
I volunteer!

ELAINE

Right. I don't know why I let fear overcome my good judgement. Len, I'll put you in charge to find other volunteers and to oversee the search. Let's not waste any more time. And, oh, another thing I thought of: Our kids still think they're in trouble, and if they are able to find their way back, they may be too afraid to come home. So I thought we should redo the arch at the entrance to the school to read, "Welcome Home, Splatt and Lara."

LEN AND CATHARINE TOGETHER

We agree.

ELAINE

Let's waste no more time, let's get going.

THE ARCH AT THE ENTRANCE TO THE SCHOOL, AFTERNOON

An adult Sea Drop is chalking in the addition to the school's sign. It now reads:

WELCOME HOME —SPLATT AND LARA
Principal—Mrs. Elaine
Sea Drop Orientation—Mrs. Elaine
Religious Instruction—Mrs. Elaine

BARE OCEAN FLOOR, LATE AFTERNOON

In the distance, Splatt sees an array of seaweed tents surrounded by a coral fence. He moves closer and observes a flurry of activity. This is a military barracks. He comes to the gate where two guards (GUARD 1 and GUARD 2) are on duty. The guards are armed with sticklike pieces of seaweed stem.

GUARD 1
Halt, stranger. Shore Drop or River Drop? State your allegiance!

SPLATT
(stuttering)
I'm … I'm a Sea Drop.

GUARD 1
Then you're one of us. You got some ID?

Splatt's mind flashes back to the Deep Drops and the threat of deportation.

SPLATT

No, sir, where I come from, we don't have ID. I'm just a pupil of Sea Drop High School, and I'm lost, sir. I just need some directions. I don't want to cause any trouble, sir.

GUARD 1

Sea Drop High School? You're a long way from home, boy. But don't worry, we'll get you home. How did you land yourself here? Don't you know how dangerous these waters are?

SPLATT

Dangerous, sir?

GUARD 1

Maybe where you come from, you don't care about this war. But this is the front line. See that sandbank there?

SPLATT

Yes, sir.

GUARD 1

Behind that is enemy territory. Every so often they invade, and we have to drive them back. The fighting can be ferocious. You'd better come in and spend the night here, kid. Tomorrow we'll see how we can get you back home. It's not safe for any Sea Drop, let alone a kid on his own, to be outside of this camp at night.

SPLATT

That won't be necessary, sir. I'm sure I'll be able to find my own way.

GUARD 1

Are you nuts, kid? If they invade tonight and you're out there … even in here it's dangerous, but at least here you have a chance. If we call a Code Red, that's when all hell breaks loose. That means an invasion is likely imminent. We have to defend. And if the opportunity presents itself, we must strike back. So, whether you like it or not, you have no choice. I won't have a fellow Sea Drop perish at my hand, least of all a kid. It is my duty as a Shore Drop to make sure that all Sea Drops are safe. Come, let's sort out a place for you to stay tonight. Tomorrow we'll get you home.

Guard 1 takes Splatt by the arm and leads him into the barracks. Over his shoulder he addresses Guard 2.

GUARD 1
(to Guard 2)
Hold the fort here and stay alert. You never know—the enemy is wily.

TENT, EVENING

It is almost dark now. Guard 1 and Splatt walk into a tent. Inside are eight beds, four of which are occupied by sleeping guards.

> GUARD 1
> This is the Guard Relief tent. There's always a spare bed here. But be quiet—these guards are coming on night duty in an hour or so, and they need their sleep. Understand?

> SPLATT
> Yes, sir.

> GUARD 1
> You can bunk down here for the night. (He points at a bed.) I'll be coming off duty in the next hour, and if you're not asleep, I'll see you then.

The guard turns to leave and adds over his shoulder:

> GUARD 1
> And kid, don't you worry, we'll get you home safely tomorrow.

The guard leaves, and Splatt lies down on the bed. He cannot sleep. A short while later, the night-duty guards wake up and leave the tent. Splatt is now alone.

> SPLATT
> (whispering to himself)
> Man, how do I get out of this one? I'll have to think of a plan tonight.

A short while later, Guard 1 arrives back with several other guards. It is dark now. Guard 1 takes the bed next to Splatt, lies down, and then whispers.

> GUARD 1
> Hey kid, you asleep?

> SPLATT
> No, sir.

> GUARD 1
> Well then, sleep tight.

Silence for a while, then Splatt whispers.

> SPLATT
> Sir?

> GUARD 1
> Yes?

> SPLATT
> Have you ever heard of Colorland, sir?

GUARD 1
Never heard of it, kid. I only know of two lands: theirs and ours.

SPLATT
Who are they, sir?

GUARD 1
The enemy, kid, the River Drops.

SPLATT
Why are they the enemy, sir?

GUARD 1
You mean you don't know? What do they teach you at your Sea Drop High School? They're the enemy because they're River Drops. They're brown and we're translucent. We just don't mix with them. This battle has been going on for generations. They invade and capture territory, and then we counter-invade and try to recapture territory. It's a question of who's a step ahead—us with the tides, or them with surge. But kid, let me tell you, if us Shore Drops weren't here on the front line, they would take over our entire sea. They hate us and want to take over our lands. We hate them too.

SPLATT
Why, sir?

GUARD 1

Because they're River Drops and we're Sea Drops.
Understand?

SPLATT

I think so, sir, but I was told there's also a Colorland
and—

GUARD 1

(interrupting)
No, kid, I don't know who teaches at your school, but
I never heard of it. But get some sleep now. You've got
a long day tomorrow.

Splatt drifts off to sleep. All is quiet. Then from the darkness, a voice pierces the silence.

VOICE

Code Red!!! Code Red!!! Western boundary!

This is repeated by other voices that spread the word
throughout the barracks. Everyone wakes up, and there is a
mad scramble for weapons (sticks).

GUARD 1

(excited—half frightened—to Splatt)
You stay here, bunk down, and keep your head low.
You've got no combat experience. We'll protect the
West Bank. You should be safe, kid.

BARRACKS, EVENING

Guard 1 emerges from the tent, as do soldiers from all the other tents, armed with sticks. They are organized like clockwork. The soldiers line up at the western side of the coral fence and wait, ready to strike. And then it comes: a wall of murky river water rolling toward them. Each soldier stands ready with his stick (like a baseball player, except that the stick is not held over the shoulder, but rather at knee-height to enable them to smack upward at whatever they're aiming at).

A voice rings out from the darkness.

> VOICE
> Hold it, hold it… h…o…l…d … i…t…   *Strike!*

The soldiers strike out in unison. They connect with River Drops and send them spiraling upward and over the barracks so as to land beyond the eastern boundary. Guard 1 fights on, gritting his teeth as wave upon wave of River Drops flood toward the western boundary. They're holding their line—barely.

OUTSIDE SPLATT'S TENT, EVENING

Splatt's head appears out the front entrance to the tent, between the two seaweed flaps. He looks left and sees the carnage on the western front, then he looks right and sees the River Drops fall beyond the eastern boundary. His two little hands appear on either side at chest height, and then he slowly opens the flaps. He sneaks his right leg out first and then his left; then his entire body emerges. He glances one last time to the western front and then, like a thief in the night, makes his way to the gate, which is unguarded. He walks out and then starts to run. He dashes to the eastern side. As soon as he gets beyond the protective halo that the soldiers have created by diverting the river water upwards, he is swept off his feet by the current, and he tumbles forward alongside wounded River Drops, who moan and groan with pain. Finally, the current becomes calmer until it ceases. Splatt now lies on the ocean bed with a score of wounded River Drops around him. He rushes up to the one closest to him (DJ COOL).

SPLATT
Are you ok?

DJ COOL
Yeah, brother, I think so.

He looks at Splatt.

DJ COOL
Who are you, bro?

SPLATT
I'm Splatt.

DJ Cool shakes Splatt's hand.

DJ COOL
I'm DJ Cool, nice one.

He looks at Splatt some more.

DJ COOL
Say, brother, aren't you a bit too young to be fighting
this … this … oh, never mind.

SPLATT
Err, yes, I mean … err, no. Actually, I have nothing to
do with this. I'm not from here.

DJ COOL
Then what you doing here, bro?

SPLATT
That's a long story, but I guess I just landed myself in
the wrong place at the wrong time.

DJ COOL
Me too, bro, I mean, like, they got me for conscription. Brother, I tell you, I wasn't even supposed to be at my club that morning—wrong place, wrong time, and now check where I am.

SPLATT
What's conscription?

DJ COOL
Conscription … that's when they get you—whether you want to or not—and they make a soldier out of you, and they tune you to fight for something you don't even believe in. That's conscription, brother.

SPLATT
Yikes, that's bad. So, what are you going to do about it?

DJ COOL
What can one do about it?

SPLATT
Well, I had a problem where I come from—that's Sea Drop Village—

DJ COOL
(interrupting)
You mean to tell me you're a Sea Drop? I couldn't make out that you're translucent in the night light.

SPLATT
Yes.

DJ COOL
But then what are you doing asking me if I'm OK?
Don't you hate me?

SPLATT
No, why should I?

DJ COOL
Hey, brother, this is awesome. Here's me talking to a
Sea Drop that doesn't hate me. This is just too awesome, bro, 'cause you see me. … Me, I never hated
Sea Drops even though I was taught to, but I never
did. And I never thought I'd find a Sea Drop that
thinks like me. Awesome!

DJ Cool gives Splatt a bear hug.

SPLATT
But I can't believe this conscription nonsense you
have to go through.

DJ COOL
Hey, bro, it's just a part of life.

SPLATT
It needn't be. I was telling you, I had problems back
home, and I just packed up and left.

DJ COOL
Just you alone?

SPLATT
Actually no, my girlfriend, Lara and me.

Splatt becomes serious as well as sad.

SPLATT
You see, that's what keeps me going. I have to find her. And no conscription, nor Deep Sea Drops that want to deport me, nor fish that swallow me, nor surfing onto the beach and almost evaporating, nor soldier Sea Drops that want to take me home, will stop me. I have to find her. And if I could have gone through all of what I did to find her, then you can beat conscription, I swear.

The Color Drop appears next to Splatt. Now it's blue.

BLUE DROP
See how much you let go of already?

SPLATT
(to Blue Drop)
Yeah, but where to from here, and what's your color called this time?

BLUE DROP
Blue, and you will find your way.

SPLATT
Stop that, you always—

DJ COOL
(interrupting)
Who are you talking to?

The blue drop disappears.

SPLATT
To the blue drop.

DJ COOL
There's no blue drop here, and what is a blue drop anyway? Never heard of it.

SPLATT
(after a while)
Of course not, I was just daydreaming.

DJ COOL
So, tell me, did you really go through all of what you said?

SPLATT
Yep.

DJ COOL
Rock on, man, you must be the coolest bro I've ever met. And yeah, you're right—bugger conscription. I'm going find a way to beat it. But tell me, your girlfriend, Lara, where is she that you've had to go through so much to find her?

SPLATT

I don't know where she is. But I do know that she won't stop searching, as I won't. 'Cause there's a place where we'll meet, and we both know where that is.

DJ COOL
Where?

SPLATT
(hesitating)
It's … Colorland.

DJ COOL
Awesome, bro, I heard some people talking about it in my club. Maybe we can help each other. I mean, you help me with conscription, and I can maybe help you find the Colorland. Cool?

SPLATT
Look, the Surf Drop Sean thought he knew where Colorland was, and I nearly got killed because of that, so I'm a bit wary.

DJ COOL
I said I only heard people talk about it. They said it was psychedelic. I'm making no promises, but I don't think you have any other options. If the rest of the River Drops find a Sea Drop here … and me associating with a Sea Drop … I can't even imagine what they'll do to us. So, do we have any other options?

SPLATT
I guess not.

DJ COOL
Are we cool, then?

SPLATT
Yeah, we're cool. What's our plan?

DJ COOL
Rock on, man. So, here's what we do. We're going to have to escape this battlefield tonight. Tomorrow they'll regroup, and we must be out of here before then. I suggest we move south. In that way we can make a wide turn around the battlefield and enter the river. There'll be no military in the river now—they're all on the battlefield. We'll have a day-or-two head start before they return—we'll get to my club and make some inquiries for you, then you can give me some pointers. I'm determined now. I'm not fighting no one else's wars, not even if I lose my club.

SPLATT
What's a club?

DJ COOL
You'll see.

SPLATT
Cool, let's move.

RIVERBED, LATE EVENING

Splatt and DJ Cool are coming up the river. They are both exhausted.

> DJ COOL
> How are you doing, bro?

> SPLATT
> (out of breath)
> I'm strong, you?

> DJ COOL
> (worse than Splatt)
> Strong, bro, strong.

They continue a while.

> DJ COOL
> (panting)
> How are you doing now, bro?

> SPLATT
> Still strong.

A short while later.

DJ COOL
Don't you get tired, bro?

SPLATT
Sometimes a little.

DJ COOL
(visibly exhausted)
Me too … like, even though I'm strong—and I'm still very strong—I think I might be a bit tired now.

SPLATT
I think we can rest then.

DJ COOL
That's a good idea.

They both collapse as though they couldn't have managed one more step.

DJ COOL
You know, we out of harm's way now. Maybe we should sleep here till sunrise. You know we have a lot to do tomorrow.

SPLATT
(relieved)
That's a good idea.

They lie down and fall asleep instantly.

DJ COOL'S CLUB, MORNING

Splatt and DJ Cool arrive at his club up the river. The club is an outside venue on white river sand. The DJ booth is close to the riverbank and raised; it overlooks the outdoor dance floor. The booth is rustic, constructed of green blades of grass, similar to a beach pub made of coconut leaves. The dance floor below is on part of a broken floor tile, which in comparison to the drops dancing on it, is huge and requires two steps to get up onto. The perimeter is secured by a piece of fishing line lying on the sand. At the far end, beyond the dance floor, the line is still attached to a giant-sized hook. The fishing line is propped up by a single pole—a burnt matchstick—to make the entrance. Above the entrance is a sign reading "DJ COOL'S." Young drops are rocking on the dance floor to music that comes from an a capella group in the DJ box.

Splatt and DJ Cool arrive at the entrance, which is manned by a large drop (BREAKER), with a deep husky voice and a face that clearly shows a lack of intelligence.

BREAKER
Hey, Boss, you back so soon? We musta kicked them Sea Drops proper.

DJ COOL
How many times have I told you, Breaker, not to call me "boss?"

Breaker laughs sheepishly.

DJ COOL
This is a very good friend of mine, Splatt. I want you to treat him VIP, understand?

BREAKER
Sure, Boss. Morning, Mister Splatt.

Breaker presents his right hand to shake Splatt's. Splatt takes his hand and with his left he pats Breaker on the back of the shoulder.

SPLATT
Not Mister Splatt, buddy. Just Splatt, OK?

BREAKER
(proudly)
OK … Splatt.

They walk toward the DJ booth.

DJ COOL

I don't know how you did that—he refuses to call me anything but Boss. Let's go to my office, it's quieter there. Then we can talk.

Splatt follows DJ Cool round the dance floor toward the DJ booth. From the dance floor, many of the dancing drops wave a hearty hello to DJ Cool, and he reciprocates. A very funky and well-built drop (RORY) greets DJ Cool. DJ Cool gestures him over and whispers something in his ear. The three then make their way to DJ's office, situated behind the DJ booth.

DJ COOL'S OFFICE, MORNING

DJ Cool shuts the door, and the noise is dampened.

DJ COOL
Rory, I'd like you to meet one of my very good friends, Splatt.

Splatt and Rory shake hands. They sit down, DJ behind his rock desk and the other two on river pebbles that improvise as chairs.

DJ COOL
(to Rory)
Hey bro, we need some information, and I reckon you're the right guy. I mean, you're a happening dude, right?

RORY
Fully.

DJ COOL
And you know stuff, right?

RORY
Fully, bro.

DJ COOL
See, my friend here, Splatt, he seriously needs to know something, man. And I've heard talk about it, but I don't know where to point him. See, Splatt needs to find the Colorland, and fast.

Silence for a while, then Rory responds.

RORY
Hey, I know stuff, but that's serious, man. I mean I've never been. There's only one person I know of that has.

DJ COOL
Who's that?

RORY
Sorry, man, it's sort of a secret, and there's a silent agreement not to talk about it.

SPLATT
(to Rory)
Rory, I know you don't know me, but please, just hear me out.

RORY
No harm in listening, but I'm telling you now, I can't say.

SPLATT
Thanks. I tell you—just listening to you, I can just see that you're a man of your word. And I think that's

cool, and I know it didn't just happen for you, man; you had to choose to be this way. So, what I'm saying is that you choose honor above lies. And that's cool, you choose right. But I want to ask you something: would you rather keep your word to some unspoken pact, or would you rather break this promise you never actually made if you knew you could possibly save a life? You got to believe me, this is a matter of life and death. I must find Colorland. It's life or death. Will you help me … please?

DJ COOL
(to Rory)
And bro, if you help Splatt, you have our word that we won't say who we got the information from.

Rory thinks for a while.

RORY
You know I would normally never have done this, but the way you put it, Splatt … I feel that I must tell you. … Amy has been there, but you can't tell her I said so.

SPLATT
Of course I won't.

DJ COOL
Amy? Shucks.

SPLATT
Why? What's with Amy?

DJ COOL
Nothing. (then to Rory) Is she here—Amy?

RORY
I saw her arrive just before we came in here.

SPLATT
Hey Rory, thanks a lot. You did the right thing. Thanks again.

DJ COOL'S CLUB, MORNING

Splatt and DJ Cool are watching the dance floor.

> DJ COOL
> Don't look now, but there she is, the pretty one, eleven o'clock.

Splatt casually turns and then spots her (AMY). She's absolutely drop-dead gorgeous, and she dances provocatively. She has at least four suitors in attendance, dancing with her and all competing for her attention.

> SPLATT
> Oh, no, this is impossible. How does one get close to her?

> DJ COOL
> Are you kidding me? You seem to have forgotten that I'm DJ Cool and I own this joint, bro.

DJ Cool catches Amy's eye and beckons her over. She slinks over sexily.

> AMY
> (with seductive voice to DJ Cool)

Hi, baby, back from playing war games? And who's this cutie?

She pinches Splatt's cheek. He is embarrassed.

DJ COOL
This is Splatt, an old bro of mine.

DJ Cool leans over to Amy and cups his hand over her ear.

DJ COOL
(whispering)
He's an adventurer like you—been everywhere, done everything. Cool, hey?

Amy sizes Splatt up.

AMY
(to Splatt)
Want to dance, cutie?

SPLATT
My name's not "cutie," and no I don't want to dance. I want to know if you—

DJ kicks Splatt in the leg.

DJ COOL
(in Splatt's ear)
BE COOL, DUDE, else you'll go nowhere with her.

AMY
(to Splatt)
You want to know what?

SPLATT
I want to know if you don't get bored of the attention
these boys give you.

Silence.

AMY
(to Splatt)
DJ Cool tells me you've been around—that you've
seen and done it all.

SPLATT
I suppose.

AMY
Bet I know of one place you haven't been.

SPLATT
And that is?

Amy pulls Splatt closer, with her face right up against his.

AMY
Ever heard of psychedelic, cutie?

Splatt's eyes light up.

SPLATT
Sure I have, it's just that where I come from, it's called Colorland. I've just been so busy with what I do that I haven't had time, but it's next on my list.

AMY
So, when are you going to party?

SPLATT
I'm ready when you are.

AMY
How about now? And how about we party together?

SPLATT
That's cool by me, but I promised my man here, DJ Cool, that I'd help him with some stuff, so if you give me an hour or so, then we can … party.

AMY
I'll be right here, waiting.

Splatt turns, grabs DJ Cool by the arm, and pulls him toward the office.

DJ COOL'S OFFICE, MORNING

Splatt and DJ Cool enter the office and close the door.

DJ COOL
Looks like she likes you, bro.

Splatt ignores the comment.

SPLATT
She knows the way to the Colorland—that's all that matters.

DJ COOL
Rock on, brother.

SPLATT
Listen to me. I could have already been on my way, but we had an agreement that we would help each other. And so, firstly, thanks so much. Without you I don't know how I would have found the way. And secondly, my part of the bargain—remember … conscription?

DJ COOL
Oh, no, bro, don't remind me.

SPLATT

You must face it, sooner rather than later. Now, all I can do is offer you advice. I was in lots of trouble back home, and I ran away. The truth is, before I was in trouble, I thought a lot about Colorland. And all the things that I went through—I mean I could never have found my way if it wasn't for one thing.

DJ COOL
What?

SPLATT

This may sound funny to you, but you've got to trust me. Remember when we were on the battlefield you asked me who I was talking to. I said a Blue Drop.

DJ COOL
Yeah, but there was no one.

SPLATT

Well, the truth is I was talking to a blue drop. It was only when you said you couldn't see him that I realized only I could see him. He's been with me on my travels since day one. And even though he never gives me specific advice, he always seems to know the way forward for me. So, what I'm trying to say is—and I don't even know if I'm right—but you need to find what I've got: something like a nonconscription drop. Man, that's as much advice as I can give you.

And I'm sorry if it's not what you expected, but that's all I know to tell you.

DJ COOL
No, brother, if it hadn't been for you, I would still have been on the battlefield. So, rock on—go find Lara in Colorland.

They hug warmly and Splatt departs the office.

RIVERBED, AFTERNOON

Splatt and Amy are making their way up the river.

SPLATT
I'm going to have to rely on you for directions—I've never been before.

AMY
Directions? You don't need directions. You just have to find the right root, and the rest takes care of itself.

SPLATT
I know, I meant directions to the route.

AMY
You think it's a route, like a way?

SPLATT
Of course, what other route is there?

AMY
You really have no idea about the Colorland, do you?

SPLATT
Actually, no. The main purpose of all my travels has been to find it.

AMY

Are you sure you're up to this? It's not for the faint-hearted, you know.

SPLATT

Sure! After what I've been through, are you kidding me?

DJ COOL'S OFFICE, AFTERNOON

DJ Cool sits at his desk, staring into space. All of a sudden, he notices a drop next to his desk, lying on the floor with his hands cupped behind his head and his thin legs crossed (NO CONSCRIPTION DROP).

DJ COOL
(staring at the drop)
Blimey, Splatt was right. Are you a nonconscription drop?

NONCONSCRIPTION DROP
Maybe.

DJ COOL
Where is it?

NONCONSCRIPTION DROP
Where's what?

DJ COOL
The Land of Nonconscription, man ... where is it? How do I get there? You gotta tell me!

161

NONCONSCRIPTION DROP

Maybe you can start by letting go of the way you know.

RIVERBED, LATE AFTERNOON

Splatt and Amy arrive at where a massive yellow flexible plastic pipe comes down from the surface, with the open end above them.

AMY
This is it, now we just wait.

SPLATT
For what?

AMY
See this porthole overhead? Every afternoon it kicks in, and that's the beginning of the way to fun—what you call Colorland.

SPLATT
You sure?

AMY
Of course, I've been down this road many times.

Splatt notices an old drop with a sad, wrinkled face (ARTHUR) close by, also waiting. He walks over.

SPLATT
Excuse me?

The old drop seems to have no zest for life. He slowly looks up.

ARTHUR
Yes, kid?

SPLATT
Is this the way to Colorland? I just need to know because I have to get there. My girlfriend will be there, and I need to find her.

ARTHUR
Colorland? I don't think that's what it's called. But what you're about to experience—it's great for the first couple of times, but then you can't stop, and it's terrible, awful I tell you. Don't start, kid, it'll get you.

SPLATT
(to Amy)
I don't think this is the Colorland I'm looking for. I was misled once before, and it nearly cost me my life. I think I would rather not—

Just then the sound of a machine starting up drowns out his voice, and the yellow pipe buckles and bends. Splatt tries to get away, but the suction is too great. Amy and Arthur are sucked up into the pipe. Splatt tries desperately to hang on to some vegetation he's managed to grab hold of. But the suction is too strong, and soon he is turned upside down.

Now his legs and body flap toward the immense suction, and his grip is starting to fail. Finally, he can hold on no longer, and he is sucked into the pipe at high speed.

AGRICULTURAL LAND, DUSK

At the top of the riverbank is a huge water pump, with yellow plastic pipes on either side. One pipe goes into the river and the other into a furrow that feeds vineyards. Splatt is spewed into the furrow. He is dazed and disoriented. He lands on his back with his eyes closed. He hears a voice.

> AMY
> You owe me.

Splatt opens his eyes.

> AMY
> I'm risking my own life here, waiting for you. You're obviously not nearly as tough as you made out.

> SPLATT
> What happened?

She grabs Splatt by the hand and pulls him up.

> AMY
> Come on, we don't have much time. If we're left out here, we'll evaporate. We've got to find a root.

SPLATT
(resisting)
I'm not going anywhere with you, you tricked me.

AMY
Listen to me! That pump is going to switch off in a moment. When it does, we'll be stuck here, and—are you listening?—we'll die. You can stay if you want. But if you want to live, you'll come with me now!

Splatt obliges. Amy leads the way, still holding on to Splatt's hand. Eventually she stops.

AMY
This looks like a good one. Follow me.

Amy burrows down into the sand to where she finds a vine root.

AMY
See these tiny holes? We've got to squeeze into them.

SPLATT
I'm not sure—

AMY
I'm getting sick of your whining now. You said you were up to it, and besides, you have no choice. If you stay here, you're dead. So, you're either going to follow me now, or not.

Amy squeezes into the hole and disappears. Splatt is indecisive. The ground starts drying around him. Finally, he takes the plunge and squeezes into the hole, disappearing from sight.

AT ENTRANCE TO SEA DROP
HIGH SCHOOL, DUSK

Miss Barge and Principal Schooner stroll past the entrance to the school. They notice the changes to the arch.

PRINCIPAL SCHOONER
Look what that heretic woman has done. How in Thunder God's ocean can someone post a welcome sign to a cancer such as Johnathan Drop? She's desecrated our entrance.

MISS BARGE
But, Principal Schooner, don't you think it may have been a good idea—I mean, that it could send a message to the children that they need not be afraid to come back? Surely the parents want to see the children get back safely.

PRINCIPAL SCHOONER
Those rebel kids don't deserve to come back here. Can you not see what their rebellion has done to our society?

MISS BARGE
I know, but—

PRINCIPAL SCHOONER
There are no buts, Miss Barge. Let me tell you, it's not long now before that woman hangs herself. There's already widespread dissent with her curriculum, or lack of it. I hear she has no idea—trying to find reasons for tried and tested rules. Give it another day or two, and I will call another PTA meeting. And then we'll see who wins the vote. Our names will be reinstated at this entrance. Nothing would please me more than to remove this garbage and reinstate what was before—*nothing!*

Principal Schooner points to the writing on the arch.

WELCOME HOME—SPLATT AND LARA
Principal—Mrs. Elaine
Sea Drop Orientation—Mrs. Elaine
Religious Instruction—Mrs. Elaine

Principal Schooner and Miss Barge notice Len and three other adult drops returning from scouting the ocean. They look exhausted and worse for wear.

PRINCIPAL SCHOONER
See, Miss Barge? Look, the rebellion has even spread to the adults. We must restore order to this community as soon as possible. A few more days, that's all.

MISS BARGE
Yes, Principal Schooner.

LARA'S HOUSE, IN THE LOUNGE, EVENING

Len returns from scouting. He walks into the lounge where Elaine and Catharine are eagerly waiting. He is exhausted and flops down on a chair.

CATHARINE
So?

LEN
It's impossible. We hardly made any distance. The currents were just too strong—they almost swept us away. I tell you, we had to hold on for dear life. I can't even bear to think what must have happened to our kids. It's awful, too awful.

They sit in silence for a while, then Catharine begins to cry, softly sobbing at first, until she bursts out and sobs uncontrollably. Len tries to comfort her, but she pushes him away and jumps up to leave the room. Len catches her from behind and swings her around.

LEN
We're all in this together, darling.

Catharine throws her arms around Len and sobs on his chest. Elaine comes over, and the three of them hug. A tear runs down Elaine's cheek. Len holds out and doesn't cry—just. They stand like this for a while.

LEN
Let's pull ourselves together—for Lara and Splatt's sake. I'm sure everything is not lost.

They let go of each other and all retreat to their chairs.

ELAINE
I was hoping I could tell the children to scrap the "don't go into the ocean" rule tomorrow.

CATHARINE
The rule was right. What if all the other rules are right too? What if a fish or something swallowed our children?

LEN
We cannot allow ourselves to think like that, darling. All we have is hope, and if we let go of hope, we have nothing. So, let's not stop hoping.

IN A VINEYARD, EARLY MORNING

Workers are picking red grapes and placing them in crates. They sing merrily. A tractor with a trailer comes by, and the workers dump the grapes onto the trailer. Once the trailer is full, the tractor drives to the winery where the grapes are offloaded.

INSIDE THE
WINERY, MORNING

The grapes are thrown into the destemming machine from which emerge only the grapes. The grapes then travel on a conveyer belt to the pressing machine.

INSIDE THE PRESSING MACHINE, MORNING

From the grapes' perspective, the press is bearing down on them. As the press squashes the grapes and the liquid bursts forth. Splatt, Arthur, and Amy are ejected with many other drops. Splatt lands and is winded.

> SPLATT
> Phew.

He looks at his color.

> SPLATT
> (to himself)
> Hey, I'm red. But this is not the same red as the Red Drop I saw. Oh, no!

He realizes that, again, he is not in Colorland.

> AMY
> Here goes.

They flow in a river of grape juice toward the outlet and into a wooden barrel.

INSIDE THE
BARREL, MORNING

A huge, automated stirrer is stirring the juice in the barrel round and round. Amy, Splatt, and Arthur get separated. All the drops are going with the flow, screaming like kids on an amusement park ride—except Splatt. He desperately tries to cling to the edge of the barrel but loses his grip time and again to be swept around, until finally he gets a good grip and manages to hold on for a while. Amy comes drifting by.

> AMY
> Come on Splatt, let go. This merry-go-round will soon stop, and you'll have missed all the fun!

Then Amy disappears out of sight. Arthur swirls by; he is clearly not enjoying the ride. Finally, the swirling stops, and Splatt lets go and sinks to the bottom. Amy finds him.

> AMY
> You're such a wet blanket, why don't you loosen up?

SPLATT

I'm not. It's just that this isn't the Colorland that I was looking for.

AMY

Don't you worry, tomorrow you'll see the real Colorland. This is child's play. See there? (She points to the top of the barrel where ingredients are being added to the juice.) That's the stuff that causes fermentation. You just wait till tomorrow—you'll see a Colorland like you never expected.

Then, the stirrer starts up again, and again Splatt holds on for dear life while the other drops enjoy the ride. Finally, the stirrer stops and a lid is placed on the barrel. It is dark, and in the darkness, hushed voices are all saying the same thing.

VOICES IN THE DARKNESS

Can't wait for tomorrow. Tomorrow the party starts (and other similar praises for tomorrow).

IN A WATER BOTTLE, AFTERNOON

Lara looks like a zombie. She just stares ahead. Mary comes over to her.

MARY
Oh dear, oh dear. What are we to do with you? You look so terribly unhappy, dearie.

LARA
(slowly)
I am.

MARY
How can it be, dear? Look how content all the other drops are—I don't understand you.

Lara thinks for a while, then lifts her finger as though she has found an answer.

LARA
I'll tell you what. You people all wanted to be here. That's what you were waiting for. And I think it's because all of you believed so strongly that you were the chosen ones that you landed up here. But the

proof that there's no such thing as chosen ones is that I'm here. See, look at me. I'm not chosen, and nothing will make me see differently. I'm trapped here against my will, and I don't know or see a way out. But I'm a Sea Drop, and I need to get back into the ocean. Then I can continue my search for Colorland, 'cause that's where I'll find my boyfriend. I'll tell you, as soon as the lid above us is removed, I'll find a way to get back to where I belong.

MARY

All right, suppose what you say is true, then why won't you allow yourself to at least break your desperate unhappiness for a little while you're trapped here?

LARA

And how do you propose I do this?

MARY

By joining us in our afternoon prayers. It will ease your pain, I promise.

LARA

I'm not interested in your prayers.

Mary thinks for a while.

MARY

You know, child, I don't think that I'm really permitted to say this because it isn't really part of Purist teachings, but you look so desperately unhappy, and since you don't want to join in prayer, you may want to consider an alternative. I've found something similar to prayer that can be very useful: it's called meditation.

LARA
What is meditation?

MARY
Mediation is simply to become quiet within. The difference between prayer and meditation is that when you meditate, you don't actually pray to the Pure One. Your focus is inward. And you can do it right here, right now, and I assure you it will ease your pain. What do you say?

Lara thinks for a while.

LARA
I suppose it can't do any harm.

MARY
Excellent, let's start then. Sit comfortably with your back straight.

Lara obliges.

MARY
Now, close your eyes and try to think of nothing. Empty your mind, but stay in the present. Be careful not to fall asleep.

AT ENTRANCE TO SEA DROP HIGH SCHOOL, AFTERNOON

Miss Barge and Principal Schooner are standing close to the arch, talking.

PRINCIPAL SCHOONER
Tomorrow Miss Barge … tomorrow is the day.

MISS BARGE
Do you think you have enough support already, Principal Schooner?

PRINCIPAL SCHOONER
Sure. I know there's huge dissatisfaction with that woman's curriculum, or lack of it, amongst most parents. And can you blame them? She hasn't been able to teach anything, let alone something of importance.

MISS BARGE
(playing for time)
I think you should give it one more day—it can do no harm. What's one day to gather more support?

PRINCIPAL SCHOONER

Maybe you're right. I have to be sure. The word is not quite out yet on her scouts that she sent into the ocean, just to find that the currents were too strong for them to make any progress. You see, that just proves that Sea Drop rules are sound. Maybe we don't know exactly who formulated the rules, but it just goes to show that all the rules are there for a purpose, and I say a good one at that.

MISS BARGE

I know, but—

PRINCIPAL SCHOONER

Miss Barge, how many times must I tell you, there are no buts? All I know is that that woman doesn't know what she's up against. Tomorrow—no, the day after tomorrow, I'll ask the parents to vote—not just to reinstate us, but that we change the school's constitution so that an incident like this can never happen again. I've always been opposed to the fact that any whippersnapper can challenge for leading the school simply by getting the majority of the parents' votes. I want this changed, and I want that woman and her cronies in detention, not to mention those rebel kids if they ever make it back here. I want them put away for a long time, Miss Barge, a long time.

He points to the writing on the arch.

PRINCIPAL SCHOONER
This will all change tomorrow—no, the day after. It will change, and permanently. I tell you, permanently.

IN A WATER BOTTLE, AFTERNOON

Lara sits in meditation. She opens her eyes. She looks a little more content, not so desperately unhappy anymore.

MARY
How was that, deary? Feeling any better?

LARA
Yes, thank you, thank you.

MARY
Didn't I tell you, dear? Perhaps now you can begin to see that you are one of the chosen ones.

LARA
No way. I think meditating has brought me some clarity, and I've never been clearer on anything than that I am not a chosen one. But I want to do some more meditation, a lot more—it really clears one's mind. Tomorrow I'll do some more meditation.

INSIDE THE BARREL, MORNING

The lid is removed from the barrel, and light comes flooding in. Drops wake up all over the barrel. Amy is immediately full of life and gathers a small crowd. She leads them to where Splatt is still fast asleep. They start to serenade Splatt with the lyrics "What shall we do with a drunken sailor, what shall we do with a drunken sailor, early in the morning?" Amy takes the lead in the singing. Splatt wakes up, rubs his eyes, and stretches. Then he notices that all is not the same with him. He gets up, smiles at everyone, and says happily,

> SPLATT
> What a beautiful day! I don't think I've ever in my life seen such a beautiful day.

Splatt then joins in the chorus and dances around.

> AMY
> And the party hasn't even started, sailor. Didn't I tell you we'd party together well?

SPLATT
Rock on. Man, if this is how it is when it hasn't started, wow—rock on.

Amy takes Splatt by the hand and leads him aside.

AMY
You see that opening there? (She points at what is the opening that will lead to the barrel's tap.) Make sure you're close to that from now on. All my friends will be there. We'll be out first into the same bottle. And don't disappoint me, sailor. We don't want to land up in different bottles and be separated, do we now? Come, let's move closer. They'll open the tap soon.

Splatt notices Arthur close by and runs over to him.

SPLATT
Hey buddy, I remember you from yesterday. How are you doing? Isn't this just so cool?

ARTHUR
Yes, I remember you, kid. You were looking for Colorland.

SPLATT
I'd say I pretty much found it. And hey, Amy says the party hasn't even started. How cool is that? Hey bro, you gotta hang with me and Amy. We're gonna be out first—all in the same bottle. Isn't that cool, man?

ARTHUR
Stop calling me "bro," kid. My name is Arthur, and I'm old enough to be your father.

Splatt calms down a little.

SPLATT
Sorry.

Amy calls to Splatt from the opening.

AMY
Hey sailor, you don't have much time.

Splatt looks at Arthur and, with a little more respect, asks,

SPLATT
Would you care to join us to be first out … Arthur?

ARTHUR
Why not? You seemed like a pretty decent kid yesterday.

Splatt and Arthur move to where Amy and her hip friends are waiting. No sooner do they arrive than the tap is opened. Two by two they jump into the suction, shouting excitedly as they plunge down into the bottle. Splatt and Amy jump together, holding hands.

SPLATT
(as they're falling)
Hee haa!

Arthur is the last to go. He's on his own.

WINERY, MORNING

The first bottle on the conveyer is full. It moves forward and then stops at the corking machine. A cork is pushed in to seal the bottle, and the lead seal is thereafter wrapped around. The conveyer moves forward again to where the label is attached. It reads, "RIVERSIDE ESTATE—Red Wine of Distinction." At the end of the conveyer, the bottle is hand packed into a cardboard carton. Eleven other bottles follow quickly, and the flaps of the carton are loosely folded over so as to still let light in. The carton is then placed in a delivery van.

INSIDE THE WINE BOTTLE, IN THE VAN, MORNING

Amy organizes her friends, including Splatt but not Arthur, into a ring holding hands, as one would play Ring around the Rosie.

> AMY
> Now for the ride!

LOADING BAY OF THE WINERY, MORNING

The driver of the van approaches. He gets in, starts the van, and pulls off. The van hits a bump.

INSIDE THE WINE BOTTLE, INSIDE THE VAN, MORNING

As the van hits the bump, all the drops are flung upward. They all find this a whole lot of fun and laugh and giggle. This happens over and over again. Splatt loves it. Then, Amy lets go of the wider circle and takes both Splatt's hands in hers. They are standing face to face. She comes forward to kiss him, and it seems Splatt is going to kiss her back, but another bump sends them skyward. They embrace and laugh happily. Arthur watches from a distance, obviously not impressed. When Amy lets go of Splatt, Arthur puts his hand on Splatt's shoulder.

ARTHUR
Yesterday, in the river, kid, remember? You asked me for directions. You said you had to find Colorland because your girl—

Just then the van breaks. All the drops are flung forward, and Splatt and Arthur are separated.

IN FRONT OF A SEASIDE
BAR, AFTERNOON

The van pulls up to a seaside bar. The driver gets out, opens the back door, and carries the carton of wine in. The bartender signs for the delivery, and the driver leaves. The bar is separated from the beach by a road (Miami Beach style). It has a sign that reads "The Sand Bar" with two palm trees as a logo.

INSIDE THE SAND BAR, AFTERNOON

The bartender (BARTENDER) takes two bottles of wine from the carton and places them high up on the display behind him. The inside of the bar has very hip decor. It is done in stainless steel with colored lights, creating a psychedelic atmosphere. In one corner is a dance floor, obviously only used at night. A rotating disco ball hangs from the ceiling above the dance floor and is in motion even though it is broad daylight. It casts its familiar colored lights on the walls and everything else. At the bar, and at high round tables with barstools, the patrons are in bikinis and baggy shorts. They look as though they have stepped right off the beach and into the bar. They are drinking fancy cocktails. The atmosphere is jovial, complemented by medium-loud island music.

INSIDE THE WINE BOTTLE,
INSIDE THE BAR, AFTERNOON

Splatt peers out at the bar through the bottle. He sees the bar as though he is looking through a red filter. Behind him, drops have started dancing to the music that's playing in the bar.

SPLATT
Wow, Colorland. Rock on.

Amy comes from behind him and puts her arms around his waist. She's looking over his shoulder into the bar.

AMY
Didn't I tell you, sailor, is it something else or what?

SPLATT
It's awesome. I've never seen anything like this, and I've never felt this good in my life before. (Splatt turns to Amy and gives her a high five.) Rock on, man!

AMY

And the party is only starting now, sailor. Come!

Amy pulls Splatt to where the other drops are dancing. Arthur watches from a distance.

AT A YACHT MOORING, LATE AFTERNOON

A yacht approaches a mooring. Zooming in reveals the name of the yacht to be "*The Spirit of Freedom*." Bret jumps ashore. Sylvia throws the mooring rope to Bret, and he expertly ties it to secure the yacht's berth. He unfolds the small gangplank to enable access to the mooring and climbs back aboard the yacht.

BRET
Shall we eat here and then just go out for drinks, or do you feel like dinner out, darling?

SYLVIA
We've got so much fresh fish on board, I would rather whip something up here. And besides, it will give us something to do in the meantime—it's very early to go out now.

BRET
That's cool by me, but we must go out tonight. It's been a week since we were last on land. I fancy a bit of a party tonight. OK?

SYLVIA

Sure thing. I'll put my dancing shoes on.

The camera pans to the where the freshwater bottles are stored.

IN A WATER BOTTLE, DUSK

Lara sits in meditation. Mary walks by with another Purist.

MARY
(to the other purist)
I think she's in silent prayer. I'm sure that soon she'll be coming to our prayer meetings, and then she'll realize that she is indeed one of us.

OTHER PURIST
Hallelujah, sister.

INSIDE THE WINE BOTTLE INSIDE THE BAR, EARLY EVENING

Splatt, Amy, and all her friends are dancing. The colored reflective lights from the mirrored disco ball sweep through the bottle periodically. There's laughter from all, enjoying themselves—except Arthur. Through the bottle, Splatt sees the bar filling up with people in evening dress; all in bathing costumes have now left.

>AMY
>(to Splatt above the music)
>This party is going to kick off soon, you just watch.

>SPLATT
>(raising one fist in the air)
>Rock on, baby, rock on.

IN SEA DROP
VILLAGE, EVENING

Miss Barge and Principal Schooner are in the street. Principal Schooner is about to put a notice (chalk-written on kelp) into a house's mailbox.

MISS BARGE
Are you sure we shouldn't wait just one more day, Principal Schooner, just to make one hundred percent sure?

PRINCIPAL SCHOONER
I'm starting to think you're against me, Miss Barge. I'm convinced we'll get ninety percent of the vote already, not the required fifty-one. No, no, we must proceed with this now. Tomorrow night I'll put that woman in her place.

MISS BARGE
Yes, Principal Schooner.

They proceed down the road, posting notices in mailboxes, until they reach Lara's house. As Principal Schooner puts the notice in the mailbox, he says,

PRINCIPAL SCHOONER
I'd love to be a fly on the wall to see that woman's face when she reads this tomorrow.

INSIDE THE WINE BOTTLE, INSIDE THE BAR, EVENING

The party in the bar, as well as in the bottle, is now in full swing. Flashing club lights now complement the disco ball. Then the strobe light comes on. Splatt revels, using his arms to create patterns in the intermittent light. Amy joins in, and they dance together. The strobe goes off, and the mood changes somewhat. Splatt and Amy continue dancing.

IN FRONT OF THE
SAND BAR, EVENING

A red carpet has now been laid to the entrance, and a rope rail has been erected to control access. One or two couples are in the queue, awaiting access. A doorman dressed in black tie mans the door. The overhead sign, reading "SAND BAR" with the two palm trees, now flashes in brilliant neon. A taxi pulls up to the curb; Bret and Sylvia get out. They are laughing—in a jovial party mood.

INSIDE THE SAND
BAR, EVENING

Bret and Sylvia gain access and make their way to the bar.

BARTENDER
(above the music to Bret)
What'll it be, a cocktail?

BRET
No, no, we don't drink spirits. Do you have a wine list?

BARTENDER
Sorry, mate, only got house wine—but it's good. Comes from a local winery just up the road.

BRET
Fine, I'll take a bottle.

INSIDE THE WINE BOTTLE,
INSIDE THE BAR, EVENING

Splatt and company are rocking to the music. The strobe comes on. Through the bottle they see—intermittently—a hand approaching the wine bottles. The hand gets bigger and bigger. All the drops stop dancing and hold their breath as the hand approaches. The hand is now between Splatt's bottle and the one next to it. Which one will the hand take? At the last moment, the hand takes the bottle next to Splatt's. All the drops sigh in relief. The strobe stops, and the drops slowly get going again. Arthur places his hand on Splatt's shoulder.

ARTHUR
Can I talk to you a while, kid?

SPLATT
Sure thing.

ARTHUR
You must listen to me carefully, kid. And I'm only doing this because I know that this happy-go-lucky party animal that you are now is not the real you. I saw the real you in the river. Did you see that hand

reach up toward the bottles? If that hand chose our bottle, this party would have been over. And sooner or later it will happen that the hand will choose our bottle. Do you know what happens then?

SPLATT
No.

ARTHUR
Let me tell you, kid. Remember the pain of going through the vine and into the grape? Remember?

Splatt's face contorts.

SPLATT
That was awful.

ARTHUR
Well, that's like a picnic compared to what happens when the hand chooses our bottle. They'll open the bottle and pour us into a glass, and then the humans will swallow us. The stench and acid of going through a human's system is almost unimaginable. And then you go through a sewage plant to remove all the toxins—that's even worse. And finally, all that happens is you get dumped back in the river. I'm telling you all of this, kid, because I can see how much you are enjoying yourself. And people that love it so much here—people like you and me—we become addicted to it. And no matter how great the pain is to get here and to leave here, we keep repeating it, over and over

207

again. And in the end, we don't enjoy it anymore. Did you see me enjoying myself? No! But I keep coming back. I don't want to see you go the same way as me, kid. In the river you told me you were looking for your girlfriend or something. If you get caught up in this lifestyle, you'll never find her. Do you have any idea how much I would like to break this habit? You're a nice kid, I saw that in the river.

Splatt is deadly serious now; he's remembered his purpose.

SPLATT
Thank you, Arthur. I know I might be just a kid, and maybe you won't take advice from me. But someone once told me that the way forward is to let go of the way I know, and that has helped me a lot.

Arthur thinks for a while.

ARTHUR
You know, maybe you're not only a nice kid, but you're also a smart kid. What's your name, and where are you from?

SPLATT
My name is Splatt, and I'm a Sea Drop, and I think I've lost my way horribly. How does one get out of here?

ARTHUR
You can't, kid … um … Splatt. We chose to be here, and now we'll be here until someone drinks us.

SPLATT
Oh, no.

From inside the bottle, the Drops can see that the club is emptying out. Many of the patrons are making their way home.

INSIDE THE SAND
BAR, EVENING

Bret and Sylvia return from the dance floor to the bar. On the bar counter is an empty bottle of wine and their two glasses—each with one more sip of wine in them.

> BRET
> Let's make a final toast.

They lift their glasses and clink them together.

> BRET
> Here's to the rest of the evening.

The camera zooms in on the glass as Bret lifts it to his lips. A close-up shows him taking the last sip.

> BRET
> Let's get out of here.

> SYLVIA
> (to the bartender)
> Could you call us a cab, please?

> BARTENDER
> Sure.

INSIDE THE WINE BOTTLE, INSIDE THE BAR, EVENING

Splatt is standing alone at the edge of the bottle. He looks forlorn. He is staring out into nothingness. He sees the bartender make a call, and Bret and Sylvia leave the bar, hand in hand.

THE PAVEMENT OUTSIDE THE BAR, EVENING

Bret and Sylvia are waiting for a cab.

SYLVIA
It's been a great evening.

BRET
Great. And wasn't that wine just delicious?

SYLVIA
Absolutely.

BRET
Maybe I should quickly run in and get us a bottle to take with. I mean, it really is good wine.

SYLVIA
If you want.

INSIDE THE WINE BOTTLE, INSIDE THE BAR, EVENING

Splatt is still staring out of the bottle into the bar. He sees Bret return and talk to the bartender. The bartender turns and reaches up to where the wine is. All the drops hold their breath as the hand comes closer. This time the hand does take Splatt's bottle. The drops see the world turn upside down. Everything shakes from side to side and up and down as Bret carries the bottle out. Then they see Bret hand the bottle to Sylvia, who opens her handbag and puts the bottle inside. As she closes the bag, everything goes dark.

IN THE GALLEY OF THE YACHT, LATE EVENING

Sylvia opens her bag and places the wine bottle on a counter.

BRET
Care for a nightcap, darling?

SYLVIA
You're not going to open this bottle for that, are you?

BRET
Yes, but that doesn't matter. We can have the rest at lunch tomorrow.

SYLVIA
Ok, then I'll have a glass.

INSIDE THE BOTTLE IN THE GALLEY, LATE EVENING

The drops see Bret come closer with the corkscrew. He starts removing the cork.

SPLATT
(to Arthur)
I'm going to the top. I want to be out of here now.

ARTHUR
Not so quick, kid. The wise Drop scouts his surroundings before making a move. I've never seen anything like what's outside here. We must make sure we land in the sewage. I've heard of drops that were cast out on the hot sand—mostly by men—only to evaporate and die. If I were you, I'd hang on until we've identified our surroundings. Trust me, kid. I've been doing this for years.

SPLATT
OK, I'll trust you, your advice has been good so far. But I seriously need to get out of here as soon as possible.

ARTHUR
I'll let you know as soon as I think it'll be safe. But for now, lie low.

IN THE GALLEY OF THE YACHT, LATE EVENING

Bret pours two glasses of wine and then replaces the cork. He hands Sylvia her glass, then kisses her. She giggles. Bret takes the wine bottle and puts it in the fridge.

INSIDE THE BOTTLE, IN THE FRIDGE, LATE EVENING

Bret closes the fridge door and everything goes dark.

AT A YACHT MOORING, LATE EVENING

The *Spirit of Freedom* lies moored. Waves lap softly but rhythmically against the hull. Only one light is still burning on the yacht. Then that one light goes out.

IN THE CABIN OF THE YACHT, LATE MORNING

Bret and Sylvia are sleeping. Bret wakes up, rubs his eyes, and stretches. Sylvia wakes up.

>BRET
>Morning, darling.

>SYLVIA
>Morning. What's the time?

Bret looks at his watch.

>BRET
>Would you believe it? We've overslept. It's almost twelve o'clock.

>SYLVIA
>(sitting up)
>No way.

BRET
Yes, believe it. No point in sailing now, it's too late. I vote we stay in port another day. We can have a lazy brunch on deck and just relax.

SYLVIA
No problem with me.

IN A WATER BOTTLE, LATE MORNING

Mary walks past Lara.

LARA
You want to join me for midday meditation?

MARY
No, thanks. I don't think the others would approve. See, I've told them you're in silent prayer. I am just so happy you've found something to ease the pain.

Lara assumes the posture, closes her eyes, and falls into a state of meditation.

ON THE YACHT AT MOORING, MIDDAY

Bret is setting the table on the deck. Sylvia emerges from below with the food.

BRET
A glass of wine with your brunch, darling?

SYLVIA
Not for me, thanks, not after last night. I'll just have a glass of water.

Bret goes below to fetch the wine from the fridge. On his way back, he grabs the bottle of water that Lara is in. Then he places both the wine and the water on the table.

IN THE WINE
BOTTLE, MIDDAY

SPLATT
(to Arthur)
I'm not going to wait any longer. If I have a chance now, I'm out of here.

ARTHUR
No, kid. Let me first see where we are, then—

SPLATT
(adamant)
No, Arthur. This is the end of the line for me.

ARTHUR
But kid—

SPLATT
(interrupting)
You heard me, Arthur, no more.

ARTHUR
If you feel that strongly about it, kid … I'd better go with you to see you're OK.

SPLATT
You don't have to.

ARTHUR
No, no, it's fine.

Just then Bret starts to remove the cork.

SPLATT
Come, Arthur, quick, let's move up.

ON A YACHT AT MOORING, MIDDAY

Bret pours a glass of wine for himself, and with it, Splatt and Arthur plunge into the glass. The glass of water he pours for Sylvia has Lara in it. He places the two glasses close together.

IN THE WINE GLASS, MIDDAY

Splatt spots Lara in the other glass. She is meditating. Splatt goes berserk. He pounds on the wine glass, shouting.

SPLATT
Lara, Lara, can you hear me, Lara?

Lara is meditating. Arthur comes behind Splatt.

ARTHUR
What's happening?

SPLATT
It's Lara, my girlfriend. There, there she is—in the other glass!

Splatt starts banging and shouting again.

ARTHUR
Calm down, kid.

Splatt calms down only a little.

SPLATT
What do I do? How do I get there?

ARTHUR
You can't get there, kid.

Arthur goes to the edge of the glass. He looks in all directions. He is scouting.

SPLATT
Quick, man, you've been here before. What can I do?

Arthur turns slowly to face Splatt.

ARTHUR
It looks like we're surrounded by water. I think we're on a ship. Now if you're lucky, you can get drunk by the humans and land in some sewage where Lara is bound to end up, and then you can plan it from there.

SPLATT
And if I'm not lucky?

ARTHUR
Well, then the picture is not so rosy. I don't know if all the stories I heard are true or not, but—

SPLATT
(interrupting)
Get to the point, man. I don't have time.

ARTHUR
Well, if you're unlucky, this ship's sewage may go directly into the water, and then you can be dumped miles apart from each other. So, you really only have

one choice—you must go through the human and hope for the best.

Splatt thinks for a while.

SPLATT
It sounds too risky for my liking. I lost Lara once before—not again. I have to think of something else.

ARTHUR
You have no other choice, kid, face it.

ON A YACHT AT MOORING, MIDDAY

Bret and Sylvia sit down to brunch. Bret picks up his glass of wine and toasts Sylvia. He then swirls the wine around a couple of times, smells it, and takes a small sip.

IN THE WINE GLASS, MIDDAY

The drops are swirling around the glass. Splatt desperately tries to cling to the side every time Lara's glass comes by, but the glass is too slippery and he loses his grip every time. Finally, the swirl slows and then stops. Splatt now can't see Lara. He starts climbing up the side of the glass to get a better vantage point. To his relief he spots her. She is now higher up in her glass. He tries to call to her again, but in vain. Then, Bret's hand folds around the wine glass, and he lifts it to his lips. Splatt is now in danger of being swallowed since he's so high up. As Bret drinks, Splatt is washed toward Bret's mouth. He frantically tries to swim upstream … but in vain. He is sucked toward Bret's mouth, and fast. As he passes over the rim of the glass to plunge into Bret's mouth, he manages somehow to get hold of, and hold onto, the brim. His entire body is swiveling in Bret's mouth and he clings to the brim for dear life. Then the flow becomes less, and Splatt just manages to get back in the wine glass before Bret's upper lip comes down on it. Splatt is now desperate. He quickly scouts to see if he can still see Lara—she's there, but still dangerously high up in the water glass.

SPLATT
(to himself)
What now?

Then the Color Drop appears. This time he's violet in color.

VIOLET DROP
Maybe it's time to let go of even more of the way you know.

SPLATT
Like what? Quickly, I don't have time. This is a crisis.

VIOLET DROP
Let go of everything—*everything.*

SPLATT
Everything? You don't mean … evaporation? No!

VIOLET DROP
You'll know the way.

The Color Drop disappears. Splatt thinks for only a moment. He then dashes to where he can see Arthur.

SPLATT
Arthur, I got no time. I just want to say goodbye. I'm out of here.

ARTHUR
Wise decision, kid, I hope you're not dropped miles apart.

SPLATT
No, Arthur, I'm going to the surface—I'm going to evaporate.

ARTHUR
No, Splatt. You'll die!

SPLATT
No, I won't. Trust me.

Amy appears next to them.

AMY
I didn't mean to eavesdrop, but why don't you stay, sailor? We can party together another day.

Splatt looks at her in disbelief, as though she should have known what his quest was all about.

SPLATT
I'm not your sailor. I'm not the person you've seen these last days. Sorry.

Splatt turns to Arthur.

SPLATT
Cheers, my friend. Wish me luck, as I do you.

Splatt swims to the surface. He lies there, and slowly he disappears.

OUTSIDE THE WINE GLASS, MIDDAY

Splatt's form starts appearing above the surface. Finally, the whole of him is visible. He is now much larger (half the size of the wine glass) and gaseous and transparent. He tries to feel his body with his hand, but his hand goes right through his body. His stern face slowly lightens up, then he punches the air in triumph.

SPLATT
I'm alive. I'm alive!

Now, as swift as the wind, he travels to Lara's glass. He locates her. He attempts to bang on the glass, but his gaseous form has no impact on the hard glass barrier. He shouts.

SPLATT
Lara, Lara!!!

But Lara is in meditation. Splatt is frantic.

INSIDE THE GLASS OF
WATER, MIDDAY

Mary tiptoes to where Lara is meditating. (Very, very faintly, Splatt's calls can be heard in the background.) Mary turns her head as though she heard something, but then decides it was nothing and tiptoes past. Splatt's calling is getting even fainter as she walks away. Then she stops and turns her head—this time she's sure she heard something. She moves back toward Lara. Splatt's shouting is now more frantic but still almost inaudible. Mary looks behind Lara. She can't seem to find the source of the sound. Then she looks outside the glass. At first, she's not sure. Then she does a double take.

OUTSIDE THE WATER GLASS, MIDDAY

Sylvia now moves to pick up her water glass. Her hand is coming closer. Splatt fears she'll crush him, as she is about to clench her hand around the glass. He braces himself, expecting the worst. But Sylvia's fingers miss him, and Splatt lands between them. Sylvia lifts the glass to her mouth, and Splatt watches in agony as tens of praying purists ahead of Lara vanish into Sylvia's mouth. Then, at the last minute, just when Lara is about to disappear, Sylvia closes her mouth and puts her glass down.

Splatt is now shouting at Mary; he is even more frantic.

> SPLATT
> Hey, you, can you hear me?

Mary hears it and looks around but does not see Splatt.

> SPLATT
> (thinking Lara is asleep)
> Wake Lara up!!!!! Quickly!!

Mary is sure she heard Splatt's cries, and although she has not seen him, she answers.

MARY
I can't. She's meditating.

SPLATT
You've got to listen to me. Please, look at me.

Mary peers out to where Splatt is, then she sees his faint outline. Immediately she drops to her knees, obviously thinking that Splatt is a messenger from beyond. Splatt instantly sums up the situation.

SPLATT
You must wake Lara up, *now!!*

Mary rushes over to Lara and shakes her by the shoulder. Lara opens her eyes. She sees Splatt.

LARA
Am I dreaming, Mary? Am I dead?

MARY
No, dearie, it's a miracle.

Lara runs over, closer to the edge of the water glass, where Splatt is.

SPLATT
You've got to listen to me. *You have to trust me, Lara.* You're in a dangerous place. A human is going to swallow you just now. You must rise to the surface.

LARA
But I'll evaporate.

SPLATT
(slowly and purposefully)
Lara, you have to trust me, Lara. You won't die. See? I'm alive. Come up, Lara.

Lara is not sure, but nevertheless starts moving toward the surface.

SPLATT
That's right. Keep going.

Mary looks on in utter amazement. Finally, Lara reaches the surface. Just then Sylvia reaches for her glass. Lara evaporates just as she's about to enter Sylvia's mouth.

OUTSIDE THE WINE GLASS, MIDDAY

Splatt and Lara embrace. They don't let go of each other. A soft breeze carries them away from the yacht—upward and seemingly away from all their troubles. They finally let go of each other and start frolicking freely, laughing and playing in their newfound freedom. They look down and see the small village, the river, the moored yachts, the beach with the sunbrellas, and the vineyard.

SPLATT
Look there, see where the waves are breaking? I moved from there to the river mouth, then up the river, through those vines, and … Oh, Lara, I have so much to tell you.

As they float along in the wind, Splatt is ahead of Lara. She trails behind him.

LARA
(excited)
Splatt, you're changing color!

Splatt looks at himself and confirms.

SPLATT
No way. I'm red!

Then he looks at Lara behind him. She is also turning red.

SPLATT
You too, Lara!

Splatt looks ahead of himself and sees the Red Drop with his hands cupped behind his head. He turns to Lara and excitedly shouts.

SPLATT
Look!

But he is too late. As he approaches the Red Drop, his body absorbs the Red Drop. They merge and become one.

SPLATT
Did you see that?

LARA
See what?

SPLATT
The Red—

LARA
(interrupting)
Splatt! You're changing color again.

Splatt looks to see his color go from bright red to bright orange to bright yellow. He looks behind himself and sees the same happening to Lara. When he turns to look ahead, he sees a yellow drop, and again he merges with the yellow drop.

> LARA
> (from behind and still laughing excitedly)
> This is amazing, incredible!

Splatt now becomes blue and absorbs the blue drop. Then he changes to indigo and finally to violet. The violet drop manages one sentence before it merges with Splatt.

> VIOLET DROP
> (laughing)
> Finally, we let go of everything.

Lara is still blue; she's just moving into indigo. Now she shouts.

> LARA
> Splatt, we found Colorland. Yee-haw!

Splatt turns to see Lara change to violet.

> SPLATT
> No Lara, we didn't find Colorland. Color was inside of us all the time. We are only discovering this now. We are color!

The camera zooms out to reveal a rainbow. Splatt and Lara had drifted through a rainbow. They emerge from the violet and are transparent again.

SPLATT'S HOUSE, IN THE LOUNGE, LATE AFTERNOON

Lionel sits at a desk. He is writing a letter. We hear Lionel's voice as he drafts his letter.

LIONEL
My dearest Elaine,

I'm writing you to tell you that I'm so sorry for how I've behaved, not only about Jonathan, but also in general to you. I've had a lot of time to think, and I realize that I have been so wrong over the years. I was just too stubborn, and too caught up in my domineering ways to see it. I hope you can find it in your heart to forgive me. I miss you, and I miss Jonathan. I want us to be a family again, and I promise I'll change. Will you give me one more chance? I truly am so sorry.

Lionel folds the letter and gets up. He heads for the front door.

IN SEA DROP VILLAGE, LATE AFTERNOON

Lionel emerges from his front door. He walks up the road to Lara's house. He comes to the mailbox. He hesitates. Then he decides not to post the letter. He turns and walks home. On the way he passes Principal Schooner walking in the other direction.

> PRINCIPAL SCHOONER
> Hello Lionel, ready for tonight's PTA meeting?

Lionel stops. He thinks a while, then replies.

> LIONEL
> I'm ready, more ready than you know.

> PRINCIPAL SCHOONER
> Good one, see you tonight then.

Lionel turns again and posts the letter at Lara's House.

FLOATING IN THE AIR, LATE AFTERNOON

Splatt and Lara are floating effortlessly. They are lying on their backs. Splatt now has the exact posture that the Color Drops had—his hands cupped behind his head and his thin legs crossed. Behind them, the sky is grey and ominous with thunderclouds building.

SPLATT
(very relaxed)
And that's how I ended up in the glass next to yours.

LARA
That's an incredible story. Mine is much less adventurous. I landed amongst some Reef Drops—they're very unfriendly. I actually thought I had found Colorland, but I hadn't. Then the next day, I got sucked into a desalinator, much like you being sucked into that water pump. Except I moved through all these filters that removed all the salt from me, and then I landed in a water bottle where I was trapped. Had it not been for Mary—you know, that old drop whose attention you got in the water glass—it would have

been even more terrible. She taught me to meditate, and that made my capture more bearable. And then I guess I was poured into the glass, and Mary called me from meditation—

Suddenly the sky lights up as lightning strikes.

LARA
What was that?

SPLATT
I don't know. Never seen it before.

Then comes the thunder that follows lightning. Splatt and Lara look at each other. They are frightened.

LARA
Thunder God?

The wind gusts and separates them a bit. Splatt struggles to Lara.

SPLATT
(panicked)
We're not going to be separated again, Lara. Let's hold on like this.

Splatt shows her how—they hold onto each other's forearms with both hands. They face each other like skydivers. Then a mighty strong gust of wind takes them.

SPLATT
Hold on!!!!!

They tumble and turn but manage to hold on to each other as they're buffeted in all directions.

IN FRONT OF LARA'S HOUSE, DUSK

Elaine, Len and Catharine emerge from the front door. They pass the mailbox where Lionel had dropped his letter but do not check for mail. They're on their way to the PTA meeting.

> ELAINE
> I so wish Lionel could have been on our side tonight. You may not believe it, but when we first met, he was a kind and gentle man. I just don't know how he could have changed so much over the years. I could do with a strong arm beside me to rely on tonight. I just can't see us winning the vote, and who knows what kind of revenge Principal Schooner might conjure up.

They arrive at the school and enter the hall.

SCHOOL HALL, DUSK

The school hall is packed, and the tension is high. Parents are talking and debating amongst themselves. Elaine and company enter. A hush falls on the audience. They walk up to the stage and take their places on the left. Principal Schooner and Miss Barge are on the right.

IN A THUNDERSTORM, EVENING

Splatt and Lara are being tossed around violently. There's thunder and lightning all around them. They manage to hold onto each other—just barely.

LARA
(shouting above the wind noise and thunder)
It's Thunder God, He's going to punish us now.

SPLATT
Lara, listen to me. You have to trust me. We let go of almost everything they taught us at Sea Drop High, and now we must let go of the idea of Thunder God. Just trust me and do it. I don't know what will happen. I don't know what will become of us. I know only this: we have to let go.

Lara closes her eyes.

SPLATT
(excited)
Lara, we're shrinking. Look! And we're falling—we're falling back to the ocean—look!

Lara opens her eyes. She sees that she and Splatt have condensed back into drop form and that they're falling. They pick up speed. The wind noise becomes deafening. They're still in their skydiving hold.

SPLATT
(barely above the wind noise)
Hold on, Lara. Hold on!

Then, they splat down onto the ocean. This breaks their hold on each other. They bounce once and then fall back to the surface—separated. They are knocked unconscious and start to sink.

SCHOOL HALL, EVENING

Principal Schooner is addressing the audience.

PRINCIPAL SCHOONER

Good evening, parents. Tonight is a turning point in the history of us Sea Drops. A milestone will be reached here tonight for each and every one of us. When we last met, you voted overwhelmingly for that woman (he points at Elaine). And I do not blame you for it, because we have all—at one stage or another—been blinded by evil. But tonight, tonight you have a chance to redeem yourselves, to destroy evil once and for all. Let us start by asking ourselves what has happened in our society since that woman took over. One: we stopped educating our children altogether—yes, altogether. You see, she changed Sea Drop High School's curriculum from a tried and tested traditional values system to … to what? To nothing—nothing I tell you. Our children have not had a single instructional lesson. No. All they've had was "Why should we hold onto our traditional values? We don't know!" Our whole educational system has succumbed to anarchy under that woman. I ask this: if we don't educate our children, what kind of adult society will we have when they grow up?

OCEAN, EVENING

Splatt and Lara are sinking in total silence—they are unconscious.

SCHOOL HALL, EVENING

Principal Schooner continues.

PRINCIPAL SCHOONER

Parents, I said tonight will be a milestone. And it will, because I am certain that each and every one of you will agree that we cannot allow what has happened to happen again. Are we simply voting to reinstate our traditional values education? No. I know that many of you see tonight's vote as that. But in addition, I am going to ask you to support me in a motion that will prevent these unfortunate events from ever happening again—ever! How much time have we lost while that woman was at the head of this school? Can we afford to lose time like this? No! How can we prevent this from ever happening again? I'll tell you: tonight I'm going to ask you to vote for a change in the constitution itself of our fine school.

OCEAN, EVENING

Splatt and Lara are still sinking in silence. They are now approaching the ocean floor.

SCHOOL HALL, EVENING

Principal Schooner continues.

PRINCIPAL SCHOONER

Yes, parents, a change in the constitution—this is the only way that we'll stop people like that woman from infesting our society with evil. I propose we amend our constitution to ensure that only our traditional values will be taught in this school. And I further propose that we amend the constitution to prevent anyone from gaining control of our education by a majority vote. Lastly, I want you vote to extend the punishment and detention meant for students to include the parents of students. We cannot, as a society, allow a minority of parents to teach evil at home, only to have their children come and spread the evil word among the rest of the children.

OCEAN FLOOR, EVENING

Splatt and Lara land on the ocean floor with a thud. Splatt opens his eyes. Immediately he scouts around for Lara. He sees her not too far off and sighs a huge sigh of relief. He runs over to her.

> SPLATT
> Lara, are you all right, Lara?

Lara opens her eyes.

> LARA
> Where are we? What happened?

> SPLATT
> We're back in the ocean. Remember? The thunder?

> LARA
> Oh, yes. You were right, Splatt, there's no such thing as Thunder God—just thunder. Oh, Splatt!

They embrace.

SCHOOL HALL, EVENING

Principal Schooner continues.

PRINCIPAL SCHOONER
So, proud parents, this is what I propose, and I know
you'll do what's right. And now, no matter how against
my grain it may be, I will offer an opportunity to that
woman to speak. After all, we are a democracy.

Elaine steps closer to the front of the podium, but then the
crowd starts booing her. She tries to speak, but the booing
drowns out her voice.

PRINCIPAL SCHOONER
(raising his hand to quiet the crowd)
The parents of Sea Drop High have spoken. Now it
is time to cast your votes.

OCEAN FLOOR, EVENING

LARA
Where to from here, Splatt?

SPLATT
Remember me telling you about my friend Arthur?

LARA
Yes.

SPLATT
Well, he gave me some good advice. He said that the wise drop scouts his surroundings before making a move. So, let's scout and see. But remember, if there's any form of danger—currents, fish, or anything else—we immediately lock arms like before, right?

LARA
Right.

Splatt helps Lara to her feet, and they walk toward a clump of rocks in the distance. It is dark, and progress is slow. They reach the rocks. Splatt does a second take.

SPLATT
(with reserved excitement)
Lara, I think I know this place. Yes, yes, this is where
I found the Ink Fish.

SCHOOL HALL, EVENING

PRINCIPAL SCHOONER

Let us vote. All in favor …

OCEAN FLOOR, EVENING

Splatt and Lara see the welcome sign on the arch.

LARA
Look Splatt, look!

They stand there for a moment mesmerized, then Splatt notices there's activity in the school hall.

SPLATT
Lara, there's something going on in the school hall.

SCHOOL HALL, EVENING

PRINCIPAL SCHOONER
… of my proposals … raise your right—

The door at the back of the hall bursts open, and Splatt and Lara enter. The entire audience turns to look at them in utter silence. Elaine rushes off the stage and hugs Splatt as though she'll never let go, sobbing tears of joy. Catharine and Len also rush over, and they all embrace passionately in a group hug. Lionel gets up and takes two steps toward them, then changes his mind and takes his seat again. There is hushed mumbling in the audience.

PRINCIPAL SCHOONER
(with raised voice)
Let us vote now!

Elaine rushes back onto the stage.

ELAINE
I say let the kids talk before we vote. Let's hear what they have to say.

PRINCIPAL SCHOONER
Under no circumstances!! I say we vote now. All in favor—

Lionel jumps from his chair and rushes up on stage.

LIONEL
(addressing the audience)
I am Lionel, the father of Jonat… Splatt. I … I made huge mistakes in my life, and I'm paying for them now. I lost my kid, and also my wife. But I'm sure as hell not going to lose my soul too. And I'm telling you—all of you—that we'll lose our souls if we don't let the kids talk. Principal Schooner here says "under no circumstances"—why? What is he afraid of? A kid? I have been one of the most loyal supporters of traditional values for years, but of late I've had my doubts. And maybe you, too, will forever have doubts if you don't allow the kids to tell their side. Don't lose your souls, ladies and gentlemen. Let the kids talk.

Elaine looks at Lionel. Tears are streaming down her face. Lionel walks over to her and embraces her. From the audience, a single voice says,

VOICE
I say, let the kids talk.

Then another voice, and another. Splatt and Lara slowly walk toward the stage. Splatt takes the stage.

SPLATT

Good evening, all. There's a big welcome sign at the entrance welcoming us back, but that's clearly not what's going on here. In any event, thank you. You'll never know how good it feels to be back. I heard talk of traditional values, and I assume this is what this meeting is all about. But before I address traditional values, let me just say this:

For those of you who said, "let the kids talk," Lara and I are kids no longer. Our experiences have matured us beyond what you may imagine. We are indeed fully fledged adult drops, and may I add that even though we are regarded as Sea Drops, this is no longer what identifies us. We are simply drops. So, I'm going to tell you where we've been and what we've discovered. I'll tell you the truth about many things that some, or maybe even all, of you wonder about. But before I start, I just want to say…

He turns to Principal Schooner's side of the podium, where Miss Barge is also standing.

SPLATT

Miss Barge, I'm sorry I messed your greenboard up. But it was a good thing for me, because if I hadn't, I may not have left and discovered what I did. In any event, tradition…tradition says we shouldn't go into the open ocean. And it may seem that there's good reason for this—the currents are strong and can carry one away easily. Having said that, if a current hadn't swept me away, I would not have experienced any of the truth I found.

It is fear, not of the currents, but of the unknown that has kept us in this comfort zone we call Sea Drop Village. Ocean currents are therefore not dangerous—the danger lies in one's fear of the unknown. This is the real danger. A current, incidentally, separated Lara and me at the outset—we were only reunited today. We encountered vastly different experiences on our individual journeys, but these led to the same outcome— it enriched and enlightened us.

So, yes, the open ocean may seem dangerous, but it is not. The most important lesson I learned about currents was not to tackle them alone. Lara and I perfected an arm-lock grip that no current can break. I only wish I knew this before we got separated, but better late than never. Fish…all I can tell you is that a fish swallowed me and I'm still here. It's not pleasant, but you don't die. I'm not going to elaborate on all the different drops I met on my adventure because it has nothing to do with traditional Sea Drop rules. But I can tell you that there are Surf Drops, Deep Sea Drops, River Drops, Coral Drops, and Shore Drops, and I'm sure that's not all. But, back to tradition. As I said, fish don't kill you, and neither does anything else. Lara and I both evaporated, and we were in the middle of a thunderstorm. And we're here to tell the tale. So, Thunder God doesn't exist, only thunder.

The audience is clearly disgruntled with Splatt's last comment. Grunts of dissention are heard everywhere.

SPLATT

That covers just about everything except for the Land of Color, or Colorland as it's called. I'm going to speak about it even though it is not specifically part of Sea Drop curriculum, but all of you have heard about it. The main reason I left here was to find the Colorland, even though the greenboard incident with Miss Barge contributed to my decision. In any event, I wanted to find Colorland.

Let me tell you right now, there's no such place— but color does exist. I know none of you have seen color, since at the depth of our village, color does not reach us. But I'll tell you that color is the most beautiful sight one can see. Yet, even more beautiful than color itself is the realization that all colors reside within every drop in the ocean. When you evaporate, you seem to move through a land of color, and your color changes, but that's just an illusion. The color is within each and every drop—it is fundamental to our makeup to be filled with color.

I'll tell you, if only the River Drops knew this, they would stop making war with the Shore Drops. And the Deep Sea Drops wouldn't keep their precious land all to themselves. So, in the end I found this: We are all just water, whatever we might want to call ourselves or believe in, or whichever way we choose to comb our hair. We are just water drops, and in all of us are all the colors.

The audience is now clearly divided. One voice calls out from the crowd.

VOICE
How can we believe you?

ANOTHER VOICE
Yes, just how the hell can we believe him?

This dissent gains momentum, with the pendulum now swinging away from Splatt and toward Principal Schooner.

PRINCIPAL SCHOONER
(above the noise)
I say we vote now. The kid has spoken, and he's clearly a liar. I want all those people (he points to Eliane, Catharine, and Len) detained.

The audience quiets down and is obviously for Principal Schooner and against Splatt.

PRINCIPAL SCHOONER
Let us now vote for truth, against the lies that this kid tells. All in favor of—

Then the back door bursts open again. Arthur and Mary appear.

PRINCIPAL SCHOONER
What in Thunder God's Sea is that?

SPLATT
Arthur!

LARA
Mary!

SPLATT
(to the audience, pointing at Arthur)
There, he can tell you I'm speaking the truth. He saw me evaporate. Come up here, Arthur. Tell everybody that you saw me evaporate.

Arthur and Mary walk onto the stage. Arthur speaks.

ARTHUR
This boy is one of the most courageous individuals I've ever had the privilege to meet. I have been around. I have seen many things. But never in my life have I witnessed courage such as this boy has. Do any of you remotely understand what courage it takes to decide to evaporate—do you? Who of you has such courage? Can you imagine the valor required to run the risk of losing your life to be with your loved one? Who of you would do this? I have only seen this once, and it changed my life.

In fact, this boy saved me. I was caught in a no-good cycle. I was addicted to this terrible pattern, but when I saw the courage of this boy to evaporate to save his girlfriend, it changed everything for me. I knew that I, too, had to evaporate in order to escape my addiction, and had I not witnessed this boy's courage, I could never have done it.

But I'm not the only one here whose life this boy touched. Mary here (he points at Mary) escaped a life of conditioning by the Purist cult. She, too, would never have had the nerve to evaporate had she not witnessed the courage—not only of Splatt but also of Lara. And let us not forget that Lara evaporated too. And to top it all, had it not been for these kids, Mary and I would never have found each other.

So, what did these kids do? They surely touched and changed our lives more than anyone ever has, and we now see life through different eyes because of their courage. This boy is not a liar, he's a protagonist! Actually, I'm wrong to keep referring to Splatt as a boy—Splatt and Lara are courageous adults who dared where no one had dared before. I tell you: I salute their courage!

One drop in the audience gets up and starts applauding, then another, and another, until all stand and applaud and cheer. Miss Barge turns to Principal Schooner.

MISS BARGE
(to Principal Schooner)
I'm with them. You're on your own.

She starts to walk to where Splatt and Lara's families are celebrating. Fade out.

BARE OCEAN FLOOR, MORNING

We see Deep Drop 1 and 2. Deep Drop 1 is scanning the horizon for illegal aliens. He has his back turned to Deep Drop 2. A red Deep Drop appears and is in conversation with Deep Drop 2, but we cannot hear the conversation. When the Red Drop disappears, Deep Drop 2 turns and addresses Deep Drop 1.

DEEP DROP 2

Mate, I've been thinking. Don't you think our money would be better spent by uplifting the aliens in their own lands so they wouldn't want to invade ours? After all, they're drops just like us, and are simply seeking a better life.

IN THE WAVES, MORNING

Sean is addressing his fellow surfers.

SEAN

Dudes, I swear to you I saw a red Surf Drop and spoke to him. And as awesome as our lives are as surfers, I just think we should listen to others a bit more, maybe hear some other points of view. I mean, dudes, it couldn't harm to broaden our horizons?

THE ARCH AT THE ENTRANCE TO THE SCHOOL, MORNING

An adult Sea Drop is chalking the school's sign to read:

SCHOOL OF WATER
Principal—Miss Elaine
Water Orientation—Mr. Splatt
Creatures of the Ocean—Mr. Splatt
Desalination—Miss Lara
Meditation—Miss Mary
Dangers of Addiction—Mr. Arthur
Other Water Cultures—Mr. Splatt
The Evolution of Sea Drops—Miss Barge
General Maintenance—Mr. Schooner

The camera then reveals that the drop doing the chalking is Mr. Schooner. Fade out.

AN ARCH SIMILAR TO THE ONE AT THE ENTRANCE TO THE SCHOOL, MORNING

The camera slowly reveals the writing in complete silence.

LAKESIDE PRIMARY SCHOOL
Principal—Mr. DJ Cool
Music—Mr. DJ Cool
Conscription and Anti-War—Mr. DJ Cool
Caretaker—Mr. Breaker
Physical Exercise—Mr. Rory

Silence persists. The camera now starts zooming out. As the zoom gets further out, it reveals a lake, then a river. And further still the zoom reveals a village, and the nearby vineyards. We now see the river flowing into the ocean with waves breaking onto the shore. Finally, we see North and South America and Africa. We see how vast the ocean is. A *loud* voice breaks the silence—it's Bret.

BRET
Care for a glass of wine, darling?

SYLVIA
No, thanks, I'll just have a glass of water.

274

THE END

(titles and theme song— ROCK
ON, DUDES, ROCK ON.)

Made in United States
North Haven, CT
02 January 2025

63778079R00167